Frederick William Ragg

Quorsum? The Cry of Human Suffering

A Poem

Frederick William Ragg

Quorsum? The Cry of Human Suffering
A Poem

ISBN/EAN: 9783337206482

Printed in Europe, USA, Canada, Australia, Japan

Cover: Foto ©Andreas Hilbeck / pixelio.de

More available books at **www.hansebooks.com**

QUORSUM?

THE CRY OF HUMAN SUFFERING

A Poem

BY

FREDERICK W. RAGG, M.A.

VICAR OF MASWORTH
FORMERLY OF TRINITY COLLEGE, CAMBRIDGE

London

RIVINGTON, PERCIVAL & CO.

1894

To

THE LADY ROTHSCHILD

AND

THE HON. ALFRED AND MRS. TALBOT

YOU WHO HAVE 'KNOWN MY SOUL IN ADVERSITY'

ADD THIS

TO MY MANY REASONS FOR AFFECTION AND ESTEEM

THAT YOU PERMIT ME

THE HONOUR OF DEDICATING TO YOU

THIS BOOK

FREDERICK W. RAGG

PREFACE

'WHEREFORE?' the question asked by Reason, after the heart in anguish wakes from its first dumbness, is followed by 'Whereunto?' a question that if less passionate is perhaps reiterated more. The answer to both questions is given by a Voice that utters from the dark something as in an unknown tongue the meaning of which we can guess at only, but cannot fully know. Ever since man's first rude cogitations in Philosophy these questions have sought but have not found a clear reply, nor does there seem in our present limits of existence a likelihood of answer that we can fully understand; though, as is the case with Science, it may very well be possible to obtain approximations nearer and nearer to the meaning of that tongue unknown.

But our emotions as well as our Reason have their own way of asking these supreme questions, and of seeking answer to them. And our emotions have contact with Nature different from Reason's and more mysterious, but not the less real contact. And so have also Instinct and Belief. To examine the mystery of the meaning and destiny of human suffering as if it were a matter of Intellectual Cognition only, and with Reason only as the means of search, is surely like sailing in search of a far polar strand with insufficient supplies, and with means effectual only for warmer seas, and not for the one long alternation of day and night. When at the very best we can gain only partial glimpses of the shore we seek, it must be a mistake to leave behind what may give aid where Reason fails — human instinct, emotions, faith. Whatever may have been the origin of these, they have their point to press. Man is not Intellect only, man is more.

Where arguments appear in the succeeding pages I do not put them forward as claiming to be final: few arguments probably can have such claim. But I intend them to speak with cogency those thoughts which the heart's hunger feels as pangs, and to speak them in the way in which they present themselves to Poesy. To Philosophy they come in somewhat different garb. The characters pourtrayed will as I trust be found modelled with reference to the truth of natural form, but yet their clay I also trust has felt the impress of the Ideality which ennobles fiction as it ennobles sculpture; Ideality which only consents to give shape to evil in so far as it is needed to bring out or to bring forth good; scorning as she does to mould the unregenerate mud of the worst human passions into shapes whose repulsiveness no trickery of garb improves, no attitude ever dignifies, and no large mouthing of tragic or heroic mask can make exalted; and then to leave them for one only apparent purpose—the exciting of a vulgar stare.

πίστις . . . πραγμάτων ἔλεγχος οὐ βλεπομένων.

Heb. xi. 1.

PROLOGUE

LOVE grief and love and grief and love and grief,
   The fugue that through the changeful lives of men
In all the generations ceaseless rings,
And raises up to heaven its complex chords,
Not to one time, nor to one melody set,
But wrought in millioned changeful staves and keys
To diapason like a voice of storm ;
A diapason which perhaps afar
May, entering some new medium's marge, be turned,
Through its refractive change of beat or note,
To one long harmony in which despair
Assumes the timbre hope, and sorrow joy.

Love grief and love and grief and love and grief—
The fugue that *may* to other strain be changed,
Nay, *will* be changed—as held the faith of Him
Whose faith endured the bitterest assault
Of all that goads the hearts of men to grief—
And changing melt, as clouds melt bathed in light,
To love and joy and love and joy and love ;
Though it hereafter change to mellowed strain

B

Of triumph in the dawn of grander day,
It now rolls on its ceaseless notes, that throng
In roar which stuns the reason seeking cause,
That seeks in utter dark without the lamp
Wherewith the hand of faith by glimmer pale
Lights the uncertain path to guide her feet,
Else wandering useless in the dark and roar—

Rolls slow in minor movement of lament :
Grief love and grief and love and grief and love.

THE WORK OF STORM

I T was the calm of summer afternoon ;
And pine and fir unto the sleepy breeze,
Which scarce their presence noted, offerings made
Of odours, and the slumber-laden turf
Lay dreaming in the light to murmured song,
Wherewith the cicala filled its stirless dream ;
Save where the forest dimness covered all,
Even in full light with never lifted shade :
Therein the long blade, scattered here and there
In solitude, reached upwards seeking light,
And thin through effort bent its weak length down,
Enforced to ponder on the strewed remains
Which years had showered from branches of the pines,
To moulder in the sloth of long decay ;
But scarce a breath was fluttered to the blade
To stir a thrill along its quivering length.

Along the pathway on the mountain side
Strolled, wandering slow, four friends who late had left

The labour-heavy'air of Granta's banks
To seek new vigour near the Alpine snows.
Two led the way, but waited when at times
They found the others far behind, who stayed,
In frequent halt and frequent lingering, kept
By form of plant and structure, that to them
Were new.   Of these was one to natural lore
Devote, to whom each plant of aspect new
Seemed almost pleading for his watchful eye
To turn upon it and to note its kind ;
The other as companion to his gaze
Beside him lingered, caring not for name,
Nor class, but caught by form and hue alone—
His heart's love poesy, and old romaunt,
And history of the long passed years, and art :
The brush, and also that which shapes the stone
To brow of thought and limb of strength, and lip
Of love restrained and dignity of calm,
Hight Runimont.   Pale prophecies his face
Of future furrows showed in imprints dim,
That came before their rightful time of claim.

Slow upwards crept the way that to the four
At every turn and every step revealed
Some interest new, some ever fresh delight,
And even the heated air, to those whose wont
Was in a heavier clime, with freshness breathed,
Though brooding 'neath a burden heavy, slow,

That weighed upon the slumberous firs and weighed
Where sunlight glowed upon the heated rock,
On which the pensive harebell lower drooped
Than wont, and weary seemed the Alpine rose,
And even the fern which in the dim recess
Of hollow rock had nestled feebly hung
As hangs a loosened limb, hid not from heat
Though hidden from the open blaze of light.

Near where the path, from under shade of fir,
Came out to sunshine at the forest's verge
It turned a jutting crag, and wandered round
To track a hollow where the waters fell,
And spent their scattered mist to dower a rock
With sweet festoons of moss and graceful ferns,
And o 'er the rock there rose a mountain-birch
White-gleaming 'neath the dark of shadowing pine.

Here stood three sisters, listening as they stood
To the low music of the dripping fall,
And gazing on the sweet complexity
Of light and shade and lichen hue of dove
And orange, and the green of moss and fern
And blushing white of pine stem mounting up,
And grey of birch.   Adream was Runimont ;
For that seemed all a dream through which he trod.
And only vision of his dreaming thought
Seemed those three sisters at the first, and part

Of that dissolving dream through which he moved :
But when, in rearward of his friend, he passed
And met the eyes of her who hindmost stood,
Before her gaze had time to turn away,
A thrill from something in that maiden's eyes,
He knew not what, broke up his mood of dream
And made his heart with new surprise vibrate,
That caused him when some few steps on to turn—
Scarce knowing that he turned—and gaze intent
Until the winding pathway brought her face
Sidelong to his, though parted by the stream
And her retreating steps.   Then moving on
He seemed as moving onwards from himself,
With steps like steps of one who moves in pain.

    He saw her and he loved her.   Face and form
Were hers that to the throbbings of his heart
Spake with the voice with which a sea-nymph's form
Amid the dream of waters spake of old,
When eyes peered wondering into azure depths
Of the Hellenic sea, and they who saw
Or thought they saw the beauty-radiant shapes,
Sought for the cause in parentage divine.

    The voice a moment seemed to stun the throbs
To which it spake, and stun the very beat
Of his astonished heart, and then arose
Its rushing pulse to tumult throbbing fierce

That shook him through.   And then a shiver passed,
And desolation, freezing all his soul.
He stood, and looking back again he saw
That form beneath the fir-shades pass from view,
And all the cicala song was 'lost' and 'lost'
And 'lost' the rising sigh of breeze scarce breathed,
And voice of mountain stream the thunder 'lost';
Shadow appeared to chill the very sun
Into whose blaze from out the shade he came,
And all the past by sudden gap fell far
To distant dimness.   Gazing at the firs—
The unresponding firs—that gave no more
The consolation of one shadowy glimpse
Of her for whom his heart was uttering cry,
He stood—till hearing from afar the call
With which his distant friends his presence claimed,
He turned, like one asudden roused from sleep,
To join the group.
                     And now they passed the zone
Where the vain essays of the struggling woods
Advanced their ranks of stunted pioneers,
That stood, in hoary lichen tresses, stretched
As seeking with averted face for life
By bending from the wonted path of storms.

Here fell a foaming torrent, bridged across
By trunk of pine, rough-hewed to take the foot,
And on the hither and the further side

Rock-guarded, while above the rock arose
The frontmost twain of pioneers, which, white
In skeleton rigidity of death,
Stood as memorials of themselves, and gleamed
In ghastly smile beneath the sunlight pale.

Past these the way led on, and past a crag
Whose brow bent forwards from its resting mates
To gaze into the valley's distant depth,
And offered at its top a resting place
On which they sat to view the mighty scene.

Far down, by distance hushed to moveless white,
The track of rushing torrent here and there
Marked with its streak the valley's floor.   A fringe
Of trees, but broken, lay along the edge
Where from that floor grey precipices rose,
And held, far up their height, ledge-seated firs,
The inaccessible home of mountain birds
That screamed their safe defiance down the rocks.
For high above the ledges rose the wall
Stained hoar and dark by watery veils that dripped
In ceaseless fall.   Above the wall arose
Rocks lifting up in pride their nursling pines
Towards the heaven, and o'er these pine-dark heights
Rock-pastures.   And above them and beyond,
Crowning the whole with distant smile of hope,
Summits of snow so still, so soft, so far,

They seemed like dream traced on the hue of heaven.

Upon the rock the friends reposed to gaze.
Their thoughts at first in wonder's silence bound,
Until the Science-lover, ready first
With word to help the struggling of his thoughts,
Found utterance.   Belford was the name he bore.

' What distant story sleeps in yonder scene ;
But even in sleep reveals its wondrous past
To Reason's slow-deciphering scrutiny !

' The soil wherein those aged forests root
Is of the mould that was of yore a race
Of older forests, dispossessed by these
Through creeping conquest.   And the vanished race
Through the same gradual victory had won
Their hold in older mould of older dead,
Of lineage older than their own.   So back
Leads lineage unto lineage, till far off,
In the dim ages of the distant past,
They take us to the childhood of that cliff
In its young garb of lowly plant, unscarped
As yet to precipice and ravine that now
Its age reveals.   And in that lowly garb,
Foot after foot upheaved above the sea,
It rose—creation of the tossing wave—
Laid on its mother-continent, that died

In giving birth and nursed on its dead breast
The child, and in the ages long before,
Itself was nursling on the ancient knees
On which it grew to age of motherhood.

'The latest these of lineaged continents :
On which look down in snowy high disdain
Yon fragments of a lineage older far ;
Stern remnants of the shores that primal seas
Fashioned, and in their slow retreat left bare,
When earth's relapsing bosom drew them off.
And then uncounted years those pristine shores
Stood up and grew to continents that raised
Their mountain bulk, till earth beneath the load
Shuddered with age-long shudder, and let down
The burden for the hunger of the seas,
That rose and gnawed her birthlings thus exposed,
And laid upon their tilted flanks the race
Of lineage new.   Now stand those primal shores
Raised up anew, and keep their distant height
Above the aspiring of the newer brood,
And snow, like peaceful unimpassioned age,
Wreathes to concealment all, or all but all,
The tracks of bygone passion, grief, and pain,
And fiery trial of their distant past.
In frigid changelessness they dure and dure,
And yet that seeming changelessness is change,
And not immortal dower of moveless age.

Those outlines crawl from mood to mood with steps
Which have long centuries for interval :
The inmost workings of yon mass—its thoughts—
That are long torturings of stony dream,
Drag on perpetual embryo through slow growth
Unto a birth that is eternal-far,
And need unnumbered bridges for their path
From one step of its reasoning to the next,
Yet all the while, as with unwearied strength,
It butts the logic of the chattering storm
And meets the challenge of the fiery sun
With fact that must be conquered bit by bit,
And strives to guard from ravenous decay
The treasured shapelings of the far off eld,
Which it within its stedfast clasp enfolds.'

'But is it then a creeping toil of thought,
As of the labour of a sluggard brain?'
The voice of Wake arose when Belford ceased.
Wake, man of massive brow and raven hair,
And lip of easy strength and eye that danced
In light, respondent unto word of lip—
Philosophy and mind his heart's delight.
'Or is it as it seems to me a force
That needs large room and minutes that are years
For its huge movement, like an ocean driven
Through the long channel of some caverned rock.
What seems to us in Nature's action slow

Is large, not sluggard : what interminate :
Not feeble movement but the march of strength,
Secure in progress. Greater is the power
That dures and dures and dures, unspent through all,
Than that which in some thunderous moment's roar,
Spendthrifts its all and spends itself in death.'

'True words you speak, but only partly true'—
Thus Flaxton took the argument in turn,
A man to whom the mathematic skill
Of problem was a charm, whose eye from mood
Of thought scarce ever melted : lost it seemed
In gaze on problems looming from afar.
' For Time is not the measure of a force,
But Time and what within the time is wrought.
The mighty may be sudden as a rush,
The mighty may be slow as slowest crawl.'

' But Time,' responded Wake, ' resolve me first
The meaning of that mystic concept Time,
That sometimes seems the page on which is writ
Creation's process, sometimes seems the mean
And medium of reaction which affords
To every conscious and unconscious thing
Its movement's rate, and different unto each,
And sometimes seems a self-consistent thing,
The pulse of an eternal pendulum
Beating one stroke for all—resolve me Time.'

'Nay, Wake, but leave such quest for other hours ;
Suffices now the writing on the page
That gives Creation's process,' Belford said,
' Which is too vast, too complex, and too long
To offer chance to scrutinize the page
And mark its fabric.   For its characters
Take all the observation of my thought,
And stare their undeciphered mysteries
Like words of scribes long ages dead, that wait
On ancient walls the unborn interpreter.'

And here they ceased, and Runimont no word
Had uttered, scarce a word had heard, his thoughts
Had wandered from the landscape, and beheld
The outlines of a maiden's face in front
Whose presence seemed, at distance, even so soon,
Of half a globe.   And in the thrall of thought
Held bound, he listened, as it were to catch
The music of a voice as yet unheard.

Was that the roar of avalanche or voice
Of waking storm which on the stillness smote ?
To them, as new as was the scene, were new
The signs which curtain round the birth of storm
Among the mountains.   All in vain the hour
Which they in leisured ease upon the crag
Had spent, had crowded signs before the eyes
That knew not how to read the portent given ;

But now the roar, though uttered from afar
And low, enforced attention to its cause.

The air had grown from its pellucid calm
To visible, and languid in attempt
To hold the weight of the increasing murk,
And through the dimness which o'erveiled the snows
Upon the distant summits light poured thin
Infiltrating, and vapours, dragging low,
Began to dim the valleys' depth, and soon
Upon the crests behind the craggy seat
Came clouds that blotted out the yellow sun,
And rolled their thunder-threatening billows close
To wrap the stacks of stately rock and ridge
That intervalled the stacks.
                          Thus roused the friends
Rose to return, but hasted not at first,
Nor knew the need of haste.   And half their way
Returning to the torrent-voiced ravine,
Where the dead pines no longer caught the sun,
Was yet untrod, when cloud, oblivion-like,
In front rolled down the hollows of the steep,
And wiped out all beyond from view.   Awhile
Was stillness ; then a sigh titanic ran
Along the downward-driven clouds and leapt
The cliff and died.   Then stillness came again,
And then some seconds more—and from the turf
And scrub and rock and stone and withered pine

Arose a wail low-noted, creeping, long ;
That smitten cried at stroke of clattering hail.

Then howl held howl in chase and swirl to swirl
Succeeding whirled its torrent vortices,
Of frozen drops that melted where they fell
Upon the mountain side, and swept in stream
The slope.   And then anon the driven whirl
Of cloud was lit with streams of fire that leapt
From point to point and rock to rock, and brought
The crack of thunder shaking all the steep
With quiverings as of pain.
                                           In ebbs of storm
The men pushed on ; its paroxysmal reels
Rolling around their blinded sight with force
That almost swept their footsteps from the path,
Made them to clutch at withered stump or bush
Or rock, or even to lie upon the path
Prone while the frenzy passed.   At length they reached
The rock and twain of ghastly pines and fall,
And steep ravine which fierce-entreating storms
Of ages from the mountain's rocky breast
Had won as path to frantic cataract.
Here, foamless in its turbid mud, the wave
Beat the rough pine-bridge that in helpless dance
Sank, leapt, and sank.
                                   But, as they neared it, came
A rush more swollen that above the rock,

Whose butting held it, threw its bounding bulk,
And rolled it headlong down to depths unseen.

A moment ere from bafflement to plan
Their thoughts could turn, the men stood still.
        The rush
Of waters wider than a strong man's leap
Ploughed the ravine far up as sight could reach,
And, some few yards below, the precipice
Stood upright o'er the valley's distant depth.

But almost ere the bafflement was past
The air was opened as with abysm of light,
Wherein the white dead pines above the crag
Seemed leaping wreathed around with torturing flame,
And on the ground the men in sudden fall
By thunder shock were thrown, unhurt save Wake,
Who for some moments silent lay, but rose
To greet with smile the faces looking down
Anxious upon him, and to plan with them
Return. 'Lo here return'! said Belford caught
By what at first seemed mocking their belief;
From rock to rock across the stream and jammed
Between opposing crevices one pine
Of those that fell was stretched. The hissing wave
Leapt striving up but could not reach its bulk.—
A bridge—the storm's replacement of its spoil !
And clambering o'er the rock which clamped the pine

They crawled by one and one in cautious haste
Across and reached their new-recovered path.

And soon the swift-retreating storm in front
Swept crosswise o'er the jutting ridge, and reached
The valley's further side and curdled dark
Upon their cliffs beyond, but o'er their path
Remained alone in sullen sobs that told
Of wrath unsatisfied, but yet allowed
Pursuance of an uneventful way.

At last the firs hung close about their path,
And through the league-long nave of gloomy trees,
Not now aroused to spread their trembling arms,
Moaning before the wind, but rustle-filled
With dripping drops, they hasted. Sobs at times
Passed through the trees and showered a thicker fall
And ceased, and left the branches drooping low,
And storm hung silent, grown to wreathing cloud
Shapeless and undefined—a stagnant grey
Of unrepentant murk. Yet even so
One sunbeam crept athwart the topmost trees
And fired the distant cliff; then slowly rose
And tinged the snow and clouds beyond the snow,—
Then let its slow regretful glory die.

What matters dying glory or the gloom
That shrouds it round? Or even the distant gold

C

Seen and soon lost which spoke beyond the gap
Of caverned cloud a heaven and glowing sun?
Just as it died they turned an angled wall
Of jutting rock.   And Belford leading first
Uttered the indrawn sound of sharp surprise,
Whereat the others looking forwards saw,
Beside a splintered fir, whose broken trunk
Blocked up the path a little distance on,
Two sisters bending anguished o'er a third
Who lay beside them moveless.

                                    As he looked
A clatter like the crash of grinding rock
Beat in the ears of Runimont.   His brain
A moment felt the sweep of dimness cross,
And staggering seized his limbs.   The moment next
The voice within his heart was saying 'help'!
And chased the staggering and the dimness forth,
The voice which sooner to the readier three
Had spoken, adding speed to speeding steps.

Help!—but what help?   No effort drew response
From that still form, and no returning pulse,
Not the least hindrance of the cold that crept
Stiffening the limbs replied with hope.   What help
But that which bore the dead and mourned with woe?

How fair the face that lay in livid death
Even though the glory of its eyes lay hid

In helpless shadow.   Pencillings of love
And faith lay soft thereon, the silent tracks
Of whose high impress even in ruin charmed,
Hinting a past, as hints a stone inscribed
The history and the thoughts of elder time.

Who goes to listen to the living lips
Unto the keeping of her God consign
The dead?   Nay who refrains?   The hostel sent
Its host and guest ; and peasants thronged around
To whom the language of the rite was strange,
Sounds and not words—but yet did sympathy
Bestow a glimpse of meaning true though dim.
And those to whom the words were words that spoke
Recalling memories to crowd the note
With meaning, stood beside and heard the words
That seemed far-wandering from their native home.

And now above the grave the patient cross
Stands, emblem of the faith and hope of those
Who laid her there in her unbroken sleep.
Patient it stands and waits the expected sign
Which yet the unfulfilling years withhold.

Thereon the dawn that mounts to toil of day
Sheds its pale light, and from its figure throws
A shadow of half smile which touches not
The grave whose length is lit, like all the path
Of life from childhood seen, that gleams with hope.

But eve, who seeks afar in heaven her rest,
Throws from the cross the grave-long shadow laid
As shadow but of peace its whole length long.
And shadow but of peace the waning light
Of life throws sometimes o'er the past, its grave.

At morn faith-lit ; at evening sorrow-dark :
Speaks then the emblem of a hope that fails,
And at the bound of life forsakes its tale ?
Not so. It is the light that casts the shade,
The light which unenfeebled by the night
Travels in space afar beyond the night
To bring new dawn. And hope though chastened points
To newer dawn beyond the reach of death.

II

THOUGHT'S PROBLEM

DAY after day was dreary length of storm,
No gleam of sun nor glint of star nor smile
Of moon to break the clouded gloom of heaven;
And only like the passing of a pang
An opened glimpse of mountain through the gloom.
And all the day and all the night swept on
The mountain winds, low shrieking in the chase
Of swarming drops of sleet and lagging cloud,
That crept for shelter from their ceaseless scourge
Round pinnacle and into dim recess
Of crevice that afforded short relief.

Besides the four the hostel's company
Was few. A priest, and one to whom were charm
Life's lowliest essays and that mystic realm
Their borderland between unlife and life,
And one whose skill availed to cross the firth
With iron road to take the rushing car;
The four and these three all. The fifth day came,

Enforcing, like its fellows, idle stay
Within the hostel, and the crawl of time
And ceaseless storm wrought friendships else unformed,
And loosed the lips to interchange of thought
And questionings after truth, which thus began :
Upon the blank of moving mist that swept
Before the casement Wake stood gazing long.
His thoughts were wanderers in the dark that holds
The meaning of existence and the scope
Of life of man.   Across his view there passed,
Writ moving on the white of mist, the wrecks
Of moss and twig of fir by gust of wind
Propelled.   And these he noted as he gazed,
But scarcely conscious of the things he saw,
And spake aloud his thoughts, and did not know
He more than thought.   But all those dreary days,
And ever since the burial-hour, a face
Seemed gazing into his with pallid grief,
And through its leagues of distance looking close,
And broken wont and mood had voiced his thoughts.

' Are *we* no more than comrades of the moss,
At wanton torn by stroke of careless storm,
And drifted at its will ?   And is it one
With riven rock and heart by anguish riven?
And one with thought and that which has not thought ?
Is there for hope in midmost growth cut down
No solace more than that which waits the leaf,

Which, severed, needs no solace ?   Can it be
That lives worn down by cares, that tread the heart
To hardness—lives whose trodden bareness yields
Not even the lowly produce of a weed,
End but in death's more barren wilderness?
And lives there are that sorrow's winds have swept
To lie in mouldering waste, till nought remains
But framework stiff and hueless of the shape
Which was their early dower of seemliness—
Beyond the withered hope of faded leaf,
The skeletoned memorial of their past,   .
Have they no heritage ?   And all the cries
Poured up in ceaseless roll through myriad years
By human hearts will then be notes to work
Some mighty harmony too great, too deep,
For aught that is not infinite to hear,
Yet are not unto that which hears and takes,
Notes claiming recompense for woe and pain !'

   The murmur of his utterance reached the Priest,
Who near the window o'er a written page
Was bent.   And at the first no meaning came
With murmur to his inattentive ear,
But soon the sound to meaning grew, the Priest
Looked up, and when Wake's thoughts to silence passed
From words he spoke.
                    ' A problem old is yours,
That from its cradle unto thought has clung,

And clings and looses not its hold . . . to you
Comes it as visitant fresh, or does it seek
Familiar haunts amid your thoughts?'
                                    And Wake,
Amazed to find a voice confront his thoughts,
Looked round and met the light of pale grey eyes
Upon him turned.   But in the eyes a smile
Of kindness beamed, a beacon unto trust,
And waking from surprise he answered thus :

'Not fresh indeed, but frequent visitant,
For in the tangles of the mazy path
Of seeming sequel and of seeming cause
In midst of which these helpless human hearts
Throb out their joys and griefs and wander lost :
The purpose of whose being and whose death
Seems undiscoverable, do my thoughts
Search exit and find bafflement alone.
I lift the lamp of theory on the maze,
Or feign, to weave the stray appearances
Into one thought, some principle or law :
I find the weaving but a sandy web,
That mocks me with its dust and no sure clue
To track a plan that, complex, still were plan.'

And then a moment's shyness and the dawn
Of what was scarce a blush o'erspread his face,
And quicker somewhat flowed the words he spake.

'And haps like that a week agone which cast
The sudden weight of aimless suffering
As bolt to sink the bark of natural joy,
Bring back the questioning as a taunt of pain
That stings the feeble hopelessness the more,
But till your words surprised me, unaware
Was I my thoughts had voiced themselves to speak.'

'But is there other gate,' the Priest replied,
'Than bafflement for Reason seeking way
In that which lies beyond the Reason's ken?
What more is man amid the whole of things,
What more the reason and the mind of man
Than is the snail amid the complex folds
Of mountain mass, of which its feeble path
Tracks out some tiny fragment crawling slow?
And deem you man can see what place is held
In Nature by occurring incidents,
More easily than the feeble snail can trace
With vision horn-enthroned the mountain form?
Naught less than view omniscient can embrace
So vast a whole ; and only mind whose grasp
Is equal to omniscience form a plan
To mate the vastness of the mighty whole.'

'This last I hold as true,' was Wake's reply,
'But in its slimy contact with the ground
The snail pursues a prostrate path with eyes

To which their vantage horn-enthroned can give
No view but tactual. Reason soars; and man,
By her uplifted, leaves sensation's soil
And looks upon the girdling Infinite.
And if there be to Nature's whole a plan,
And if there be a Reason which has planned,
And we in that High Reason have but share
Smaller than small : or if the course of things
Have method such that Reason can translate
That method into language of her own,
As from her own not too remote to give
Interpretation, we meseems might gain
Some glimmering of the plan, and hold some hope
To find an exit from the labyrinth
Closed else to exit. Seen afar there seems,
When search in realms inanimate is made,
A gate and way that leads unto the gate,
But when the search is turned to seek the law
That rules the throng of life, aghast we meet
A spectre fronting that but flaunts the roll
Of hope and life and purpose unfulfilled.'

 ' 'Tis Reason and Feelings jointly argue thus,'
So spake the Priest. ' Reason, it seems to me,
Can in its own domain but *thus* conclude : —
"What ends has in some kind fulfilled its course,"
But then if Reason in her own domain
Can soar—though rather I should term it climb,

A volant climb with hold upon the steeps—
Still when she searches regions not her own,
With her own powers alone of search, she gropes ;
She sees but part, and takes the part for all.
And in that realm where you would have her search,
'Tis only when she mounts the chariot-fire
Of faith and gazes thence with vision wide,
That she beholds in just relationship
The separate portions of the outline vast.

' The Feelings leading Reason point to lives
In numberless multitudes as unfulfilled ;
But from that vantage point which Faith affords,
O'er widened circle of fulfilment's rim
She looks and sees the far-off light that shows
How immatureness of a Pisgah death
Exceeds attainment of a Promised Land.'

But Wake, unsatisfied, made answer thus :—
' Nay surely every tract is Reason's own
And doth not Reason, all unaided, grasp
The widest view of things ?   In careful path
To search the tracts of natural working close,
Though she from close may make her scrutinous gaze,
It is her native way where-through to gain
The view of wide-embracing law.   A bridge
She thus constructs to reach the far unknown
By step and step, assured of all the way,

And builds colossal fabrics that, in strength
Secure, attest the triumph of her toil.'

' But if she do uplift such pathway high,'
The Priest replied, ' in realms of Natural lore,
The cantilevers of her progress rise
From piers whose base is in unfathomed sea,
In depths that save to Faith are unexplored ;
For what men place whereon to lay the pile,
And name assumptions, have the name as sheath,
But in their inmost structure are Belief
Or are the closest kindred of Belief.'

At this the man of Science with no word
Looked up and steadfast gazed upon the Priest,
But listened to the argument thenceforth.

' There is such basement,' thus resumed the Priest,
' In Science even for that which, most secure,
Is steadied unto fact's accomplishment,
And in the problem-depth of life and mind
It is not strange that there is need no less
Of such a basement.   But therein the hopes
And agonies of men, and broken lives,
Impelled, as Reason is, to seek wide law;
Impelled, as also Reason is, to lay
Their base on dark assumptions unbeheld :
Show not it may be proof which counts as proof

At Reason's bar, but force upon the mind
Such weighty evidence as of Belief
Builds a conviction adamantine-strong,
As Reason builds her fabrics on such base ;
And that which unto Reason's self is proof,
Is not Belief's, nor is Belief of her,
But, both supreme within their rightful realms,
Allied they hold an unimperilled sway :
But if you disenthrone Belief you drag
The war of ruin into Reason's realm,
And wreck the homes and lands of human Hope.

'And though we know not what is unfulfilled,
Nor what has had fulfilment as in part,
It is methinks at best a part alone
That is fulfilled.   For even the fullest life
Points only on.   Still more points on the life
Whose sole fulfilment here has been of pain,
And if conjecture only gives such hope—
Conjecture—that can give no settled shape
Of plan, nor hint of knowledge as secure,
This is but as it is with Natural things.
Each bud is dowered with embryo dower that shapes
Its future, though to us the dower of one
Be indistinguishable from the dower
Of other, till sufficient length of growth
Reveals its separateness of destiny.

'The lives of those whose uncomplaining steps
Went downward from one suffering to a worse,
With scarce a smile of aught that seemed like love
To light the shadow of their gloom of life,
And scarce a clasp of aught that bore the limbs
Of pity, whilst their own hearts' altar-fire
Of self-renunciation sent abroad
Its glow of generous feeling and its light
Of pardon for their torturers : these speak
Claim for belief in something more beyond
To add fulfilment to the lives which thus,
Except in suffering, were unfulfilled.
A voice of claim that mounts to thunderous roar,
When after comes the cry of countless crowds
Crushed by the foot of human cruelty
With iron tread—not willing martyrs these,
For cause that lights the heart to meet its fate,
But simple sharers in the woe passed down
By wailing generations as their dower.

'Science to seek revealment of a law
Adds fact and fact and groups to large array,
And from the array draws forth her argument :
Thus group, nay, mass all instances of woe
To their colossal crowd—bewilderment
Is all that Reason, by herself, can give
As answer to the mystery which presents
Such awful front.   But therewith comes a pain,

·

A formless voiced conviction uttering cry,
That has no rest until Belief comes forth
To paint the life of man with destiny
In further hope when this life's sun is set ;
And leaning on Belief the fainting heart
Of Reason gains a strength to face despair.
Assumption and assumption only—thus
You term that strange conviction.   And I grant
The name.   It is assumption chosen to build
The only fabric fitted to the need—
What other way does Science tread but this?'

III.

THE PRIEST'S TALE

BUT hear a tale of sorrow that may give
Pattern of all. Perchance it seems at first
A tale that might outsadden even the sad—
It has a thousand and a thousand mates.

'There lived a maiden beautiful in form,
Whom in the woman's fulness of her growth,
The rapture of a passion to relieve
The sufferer's pain led often forth to tend
The helpless sick. It seemed that worst disease
And loathsomest was like a voice that said
Within her "Come," and with the virgin-thrill
Of pure maternal love she soothed their pain.
And when upon her native land the storm
Of war with heavy throng of sequent woes
Broke—then she sought the camp and tended there.
And ever, where she nursed, an angel's face
Seemed present to the gaze of wounded men
Half swooning in their pain ; an angel's hand

Seemed touching them in dream, and in her words
Flowed what was like communicated strength
To strengthless hearts. The dying left a smile
To live upon the silence of his face
If he but held her fingers as he died;
And whoso, in the hour when fever led
Feelings and thoughts tumultuous in revolt,
Met the command of her calm gaze and lip,
In him the frighted heart of Reason checked
The panic of its pulses for awhile,
And held delirium's raving tightly back.

'There was a day when dubious battle dragged
Noonwards its desultory length of fight,
And, seizing quick advantage on one wing
Found isolate in stress of war, the foe
Poured through masked movements unexpected storm.
So well that avalanche of iron death
Was channelled on its unsuspecting aim,
That from the squadron's head in rapid swathe
Some moments swept the leaders down in death
Save one—and he the youngest—all but boy.
But calm and penetration seemed to well
Even like clear intuition in his brain,
And give its outward sign of head erect
Asudden, and of eye whose rapid glance
Was firm in keenness. One clear path he saw
To save disaster; onward sweep to gain

Delay for others, death for him and his.
And lifting up the flag he pointed on
And crying " Forwards ! " urged his champing steed.

' His squadron read his thought.   A moment more
The fire of exaltation made each face
An altar for its burning ; self-devote,
With triumph as of victory from their throats
Pealing, the squadron swept as foaming wave
Advances from the ocean's open deep
Storm-driven to crash on some low cliff.   A roar
Of guns responsive drowned the shout.   The flag
Held forwards staggered in the staggering hold
Of him who led—but even as he fell
He gathered all his strength to stay his fall—
'Twas like the upward rush of flickering flame
At dying—closed and wordless were his lips,
But face towards his men he stretched his arm
And pointed onwards with the flag—then sank.
The fierceness of a silence sterner still
Than shout of self-devotion held the ranks,
All other promptings from their stormy hearts
Were driven by anger forth, their fury broke
Upon the astonished foe in rush unchecked
Even by the murderous rain of bolts that struck
Their path and strewed it thickly with their dead.

' Palsy and fear broke down the enemy's aim

And shook their strength, and where but now the gun
Roared out were left the groans of wounded men
And silence of the dead.   The charge had turned
The tide of battle.   Reining in to wait
Advancing help and make pursuit secure
The squadron halted, and behind them rose,
Like voice of roaring waters, cheers that spoke
The coming of their comrades, and the pride
Of loud applause—one third alone could hear—
Death-deaf in blood the rest o'er whom it rolled.

'The ensign lay, his grasp upon the flag,
Moveless but breathing still ; and tender hands
Conveyed him to the place where each his turn
The wounded waited for the surgeon's aid.
And seeing him proud lips and prouder hearts
Refused attendance till his swooning frame
Was wreathed in coil of bandage o'er the wound.

'Slow to his brain crept dim sensation back
And when his feeble thought assuming strength
Gave meaning to the picture which his eyes
Beheld, but only meaningless before,
He saw with wonder stealing through his soul
That maiden-offering of untiring watch
And patient care and ever ready help—
Symbols of selfless conquest of the heart,
And turning of its weakness into strength

To bear the toil whose loathsomeness by glow
Of pure devotion's noble flame was lit,
Even to the clothing of its hideousness
In bright surprise of interest.   Just as eve
Pours gently on some shapeless mass its veil
Of tender light, and remedies defect
Or tortured shape with hallowedness of glow.

'And day succeeding day revealed the scene
Unchanged, and wonder grew to love whose strength
Captured the forces of his heart.
                                            The maid
Received, not otherwise than as the wont
Of grateful thought, at first the signs of love,
But when themselves her shrinking feelings knew
In presence of the gaze of love, her heart
Sent forth its hurrying force to mount the guard
Of blush upon her face, then gave the sign
Which meant recall, and left the face as pale
As if it were ungarrisoned of life.

'But not a word he spake of love nor breathed
His longing nor made effort that should woo ;
For duty gazed in every glance she gave
And spake in every utterance of her voice
And said "Forbear . . . is it a time to woo ?
Thy country hath its need of her and thee."

' But, from the moment when she felt the stir
Of that new consciousness, a thrill kept pale
Her face and marked more firmly on her lip
The line of clear resolve and kept her eye
Restrained and cold.   And he, when first he saw,
Felt fear and doubt in writhing struggle smite.
As on some perpendicular wall of rock
The howling waters take their rushing aim
And falling back writhe on their rising selves :
But sternly does the rock confront with calm
That ceaseless hounding.   So with purpose fixed
His will the strife confronted.

                 And the hour
Of parting came, and when that hour was come,
Was but a moment's falter in her tone,
A moment's anguish kindled in her eye,
And but a moment's putting forth of hand
To clasp, with consequence of quick recall,
A moment's pallor ; but from these he gained
A strength which made a fortress of his heart
And high resolve of love.   Before that hour
His country claimed his duty, which now rose
In resurrection-strength new-dowered with life
As duty to his country and to her.

' Long time unequal to the invader's strength,
Resource and valour struggling stedfast on
Battled in vain.   From camp to leaguered town

The ranks in sullen slow retreat were led.
Therein, in scorn to yield, they held at bay
Their insult-breathing foe, and all the crash
And wreck of deadly bolt with patience faced,
Awaiting long-delayed relief, and bore
The pangs that come with hunger's fierce blockade,
Till man and man, as famine struck them down,
Smiled in the confidence of noble death
Bequeathing to the comrades whom they left
The hope of victory by enduring on.

'But in a night whose darkness held a dark
That passed its natural dark came on the end.
Famine made incomplete the sentry's ring;
For here and there, with arms in hand, the dead
Was watch. And from the city traitors passed
A sentry's silent corpse, and gave the foe
The secret signal where their rush unchecked
Could carry bloodless the unguarded wall—

'A dark of horrors passing natural dark;
For shriek of flying woman and the groan
And gurgle of the dying gave first note
Of treachery and assault.
              Midnight . . . and fear . . .
Midnight . . . and cry of horror, shame, and pain,
Spreading from home to home, and street to street,
And even church to church.

Midnight . . . and laugh . . .
And yell that rose from savage throats of men,
Mad in the growing thirst of horrid deed,
Spreading from home to home and street to street,
And even church to church, where deeds of crime
Profaned the very altar steeped in blood.

'Midnight . . . and shriek of pain and yelling laugh
That closed around the wards where shrunken forms
Watched o'er the sick.   The maiden at their head,
Whose will was struggling gaunt with clasp impaired
To master all the unreadiness of sloth,
That crept with famine's pallid blood through limb
And thought; and wounded men their helpless fear
Gasped forth at sound of that ill-omened roar.
But in such hour throned queen by calm o'er fear
She kept their panic bound.
                    Midnight . . . and yell . . .
A sea of howls that through the hall below
With sudden loudness broke and drowned the crash
Of shattered doors, and clamoured up the stairs.
And faces lit with murder-glare burst in
Upon the ward, agape in midmost yell;
But lip and lip grew still of them abashed
At sudden sight of nurse and wounded men,
Till on the face of one a baleful smile
Revealed some purpose dawning on his thought
That lit the fierce brutality within;

He sheathed his sword, and stepping forth he seized
And strove to whirl that maid in dance around,
And 'dance' and 'dance' the yelling crew cried out,
And started in pursuit of maids that shrank
Before the red pollution of their touch.

'She shrank not, but with foot upon the floor
Firm-driven, the eagle's greatness of disdain
Lighting her eyes, she stood.   Her face turned front
Like pale Athene's calm magnificence
Of marble scorn upon the hands reached out
To grasp her waist, which, when they touched, the swell
Of indignation rolled the feebleness
Of famine back beneath its risen flood,
And on his face her folded fist smote full
A blow that checked at first, then after roused
His madness unto more.   The oath which left
His lips made all the lips of wounded men
That heard shriek on him all their helpless wrath ;
Forgetful of their weakness some essayed
To rise in her defence, and opened thus
Their wounds anew, and fell in faintness back ;
And one, his sword arm gone, arose, and took
In his left hand a crucifix, and neared
With tottering steps of feebleness, and held
The emblem up before the ruffian's face
Who smote the crucifix, and uttered curse
On that and on the Christ, and on the hand

That held, and keeping grasp upon the maid
He drew his sword, and to its shoulder short
Sawed the arm through which, when the crucifix
Was forced from out his grasp, the wounded man
Had placed as barrier about the maid.
Then, from the pallets of the wounded shrieked,
Rose curse on curse of those that could not aid
And saw his fiendish purpose unrestrained,
And shrieks began from lips whose shrieks began
As of the sane, but closed in idiocy ;
And some in that vain cry gasped out their last.

'Calm in the uproar like the voice of doom
The near cathedral's bell pealed slowly, *one*,
Scarce heard, and heard, scarce noted in that room
Amid the shrieks.   But ere the bell-clang died
The din of clattering feet came through the door,
And when the clang grew silent all the room
Except for maniac groans low-voiced, was still ;
And the dead ruffians strewed the court below.

'For voice of doom had changed the course of war.
The dark which cast on massacre its mask
Had thrown a covering on approach of friends
That found the enemy on rapine bent
Unwary.   From the captured camp their rush
Of quick surprise tracked up the path of blood,
And cry and shriek and wanton fire begun

Were guides for those who slew in act itself
Of pillage, pillager; and rising moon
Gave its pale light to work complete success.

'And he whose heart presaged where he should find
The maid, had led to that cathedral square
And up into the ward his ready band.

'They raised the maiden's helpless form, that stunned
Lay bleeding, placed her on a couch and wiped
The stains of blood, and watched the slow return
Of conscious thought, which came before they deemed
That consciousness was near. She looking up
Bewildered saw the ensign's face above
Fixing its anxious gaze upon her face,
And staring round for help to comprehend
Such seeming dream she met the signs that brought
Distraught remembrance of the horrors passed;
And in dismay before one thought that heaped
Its terrors on her, will half lost its rein.
She sought in their denial of her fears
What piteous silence could not give. Her cry
Of sudden anguish, never stilled again
In ears of those who heard, broke forth. She turned
To him who stood beside, and flung her arms
Around his neck, and drew his face to hers
And kissed, and kissing held as one who drowns;
Then loosed her clutch, and sank in swoon that woke,

But woke with Reason gone.   She lived and pined,
And monthly sicklier grew, and in the hour
When that was born which came, in murmur spoke
The name of him she loved, and feebly groped
As one in darkness feeling lone—and died.'

IV.

CHAOS OR PLAN?

BY this the listeners added one to one
     Had grown in number, till the silence round
Showed all the room attentive.   As the tale
Came to the sorrow of its end, a sound
Not sob nor word, nor yet by mean of word
Expressible ; a breath of moving pain
Escaped the lips of all the listeners.

' By one know all,' the Priest went on.   ' The tale
In all its horror does not more than touch
The skirts of outrage crowded on its stage
By war—held secret back by hand of shame
From lip, but not from memory of those
That have beheld the scenes or mixed therein.
I who began, to end it as a priest,
A soldier's course have heard the howl of fright
When moving guns by scourge-lashed steeds were dragged
Across the wounded lying low in blood :
Have heard the wail of helpless men die down

In roar of flames: have heard—I hear it still—
The cry of shrinking woman in the grasp
Of man outfiending in his deed the fiend:
Have heard the shriek of tortured child ring out
Amidst the blasphemies of the drunken sack,
And savage laughter raised to greet the pain:
Have seen such deeds as pale the blush of shame
And make belief to stagger smitten in pain.

'If pain unrecompensed be justified:
More reason is to hold it justified,
Inflicted on those ready to inflict,
If immaturity of hastened death
Incompensate :—it should be so in those
Who hold for use the instruments of death.
But even therein the undeserving throng
Of victims in mid life cut down or left
With life-long grief or mutilated frame
Or stain of ineffaceable shame flings out
Such argument against the will that leads
Or blinks the leading of unrighteous lot—
If there be nought but present life of man—
As turns upon the heart and gores its way
To force conviction in, that something more,
Which death has power to hide but not annul,
Remains to give completion and redress
To life that unfulfilled is closed in woe.

And war owns only part of human pain
And only part of human cruelty
Endured but undeserved.
                    The argument
From these, from all, is more than Reason's own—
Is more than that her own domain can hold,
The wider-bedded rock is that which holds
Both Reason's soil and Instinct's whole domain.

'Without the hope which this conviction brings
The fairest life of man is unfulfilled,
But with it that which, unfulfilled the most,
Cries out its unfulfilled necessity
As part of more fulfilment, even in part,
In falsehood of its seeming is fulfilled.'

But when he ended Runimont began.
'But all the world, the world is full of woe,
And even with hope of compensation given
In some new life, in some far after world,
I cannot trace the meaning of its need.
There is, I know, a voice whose accents speak
The glory of endurance and resolve ;
And death with smile of rapture met by those
Whose martyred limbs are tortured for some cause,
Which they regard as truth, bears witness clear
To exaltation in career of pain
Resolved upon by noble thought and kept.

But fill the roll of martyrdom, and write
In that high volume noble wifehood's pain
That stainless shrinks, for duty and her child,
From even a wish that seems apostacy
To vows before the altar spoken and God :
And enter to the lowest rank all claim
To suffering for some royal thought, and grant
That sequel of endurance in such sort
Is filled with exaltation and a heaven
In hallowing pureness and embrace of God—
Embrace too high for mortal save as pain
And kiss of death.   And grant as somehow need
For such result, such anguish, still remains
The crowd of useless woes that throngs the earth,
Increased in some wise more by that which vaunts
Its path of progress—civilisation's self—
Whose pleasures and whose mere necessities
Have bloodless murders for their ministrants
More crowded than the blood-low heaps of war.
The throng of woes, unheeded but unplanned,
Flung wanton in amongst the hearts of men,
And seeming for no clear redeeming end,
Is heaped to countless by the miseries
That cruelty with purposed blow inflicts.
And of such corn the harvest soil of earth
Seems to continual reaping over full.'

And here he ceased as in mid rush of word.

But, as he ceased, began the Engineer,
A man to whom the toil of men and men
Themselves were instruments, a kindly man,
And much considerate of the lives whose days
Were spent in working out his schemes and will.

' For every shadow there must be a light,
And there can be no misery but has joy
At hand, though in some garb at first unknown.
Endurance has its thrill you grant, if so,
Then woe has use.   And even without regard
To compensation in some life to be,
Some glimmerings of its use methinks are clear ;
Without the spur with which it taunts the heart
Good were not brought from evil, nor from lack
Sufficiency ; discomfort wakens plan
And rouses thought, except for whose advance
Thus forced, man were even yet the chattering heir
Of mumbled cogitations not released
From swathing-bands of imbecility.
And pain is but discomfort's sterner mien,
And woe the sternest attitude of pain.
Thus where the earth gives promise, but gives up
Reluctant in the yielding, what she bears,
And toil and thought were needed to subdue
Her stubborn mood, has man to higher power
Of mind progressed through effort need enforced.
Nor other where the challenge of a path

That now is ease and now to save from death
And loss needs all resource of ready brain
Is offered by the restless-tempered sea.
And ever where is need of plan and scheme
To raise or keep a home that love with love
May share, the sense of deprivation wakes
The understanding to its exigence
And spurs its path.
    But, you will say, reward
Follows not effort with impartial step
And seems at times as fickle as unjust—
I know it—but we are not dowered to know
Where fails the solid rock of certain claim
Beneath the face of its apparent plea,
Nor all defect that spoils its written deeds,
Nor know we even how oft defeat may serve,
Used right, as means for final victory,
Nor always know when what has seemed defeat
Is but the shadow of a true success.

'But deprivation and its sterner moods
Have other roll to show than climb enforced
To ever newer heights before unseen,
Or dim attainment in the distance far.
For if in anywise enjoyment comes
It most securely comes with pain's release,
Even when release refuses every hope
Of lengthened term. And side by side with toil

E

Moves somewhat of reward—for in the end
The aim of toil attained, though it bring joy
Brings not that joy which urges to attain
Before attainment bids the effort cease—
The hunting ground is greater than the feast.

'Nor could you level unto evenness
All kind of toil, that unto all should come
One fixed result and meed. To work such scheme
Were need to disenthrone advance and place
Stagnation on the throne advance had held.

'But misery on the life most toilsome lays
Her heaviest ban, I know your thought replies,
And drags the lowliest down but spares the high—
A flood that slays the flower, but leaves the tree.
But if you speak of toil of limb not brain
I know not that your thought is fully true.

'And though the path of Progress is with stones
That are the woes of human hearts, made firm
For her advance, the need for this is less
Than it would seem. Unthrift it is which gives
To covetise its greatest chance to work
The will that lays those stones of misery down,
And that which is the surest seed that sown
Brings woe its crop is thriftless uncontrol
Of wish or passion. In itself the heart

Bears its own destiny of love or hate,
Of suffering poverty or secure content
That bids oppression kneel before its door.

'And with whatever ardency you list,
If you shower benefit of gift or heart
In hope to spur the thriftless unto thrift,
Or rouse desire in thoughtless Penury
To have within its home what seems to you
No less than need, if life be worth its name,—
Unless you hold the secret key which first
Opens the way for knowledge of the need
To enter in, you have for your reward,
The moment when in doubt you stay your hand,
As you behold your boon to be no boon
But only more incentive unto waste,
The ringing mockery of ungrateful curse.

'And evil though it seem that due reward
Is scant, with niggard hand, and comes to few,
The evil is less evil than it were
If oftenest and not seldomest reward
Came lavish with her gifts, to shower them down
On that which cares not to put effort forth.
For worse unthrift and worse than even unthrift
Would follow on unworthy wish to gain
Secure result without the mean of toil.

'You think me hard? You think perchance result,
If such, is but unnatural consequence
Of Progress wrongly pushing her advance?

'Then let me point you to the page whereon
Of old was written the death of Him whose life
Reveals as clear as any other thought
The wish to lavish on the misery
And woe and weakness of the race of man,
And on the labour-wasted lives of men,
Its unrewarded store of benefit,
Its flowing sympathy, its healing touch.

'And with what gratefulness of loud acclaim
Was He received when something more than gift
Stood forth as purpose of His life and love?
When rousing unto nobler life the heart,
And nobler aim, was patent as His thought?

'The acclaim was "Crucify!" the thanks, the scoff
At dignity of fortitude in pain,—
In that it was magnanimous of gift
That life was failure, though without such bent
No life may be effective unto good,
And it was only as within its grasp
Holding the torch to light the ashen heart
And kindle into thrill its smouldered fire,
While in the soul it waked a sense of lack

By lifting up in front the pictured thought
Which showed the glory of the perfect form
Manhood might reach ; and adding to this sense
Of lack a longing pulsed with beating hope ;
That even such lofty life attained its aim,
And chained success as slave unto its power,
Nor that, before it reached the bourne of death.

'' T is only so that gifts, no longer toys
For minds to waste with childhood's false esteem,
Achieve their due success.   For in themselves
First must men have desire and sense of need,
Else that which comes to greet them is but spurned ;
Nor is there bond at all to bind the heart
Of him who has received to him who gives,
Like that which binds the heart of him who gives
To him to whom he gives—until the frost
And winter of ingratitude, severe
With pang of cold contraction, snap the bond.

' Change all, and give a universal dower
That strangles effort ; wipe from out the heart
All emulation—and a slumbering world
Of level tracts of arid, seedless dust,
And dull, dead flat of moveless, tideless sea,
Is all the poor creation of your wand.

' I speak not as disparaging the schemes

Planned by philanthropy with heart in pain
To wipe disgrace of squalor from the world,
And pillow helpless suffering on her breast.
The heart of Progress weak without them stops
In stupor.   But they cancel not the need
Of spur with woe as point to urge to toil.'

'And yet how mean the total of result.'
Thus Runimont again took up the thread—
'The wounded in the struggle meets a fate
More hard than that pursues malingering feet,
And unto few is life a prize or joy,
But unto most the making for that few
Their prize secure is pain and woe and toil :
I speak of what the world pursues as prize
And labours even fiercely to achieve.
Such prize, I know it well, is not the whole,
Is sometimes even a thing for high disdain,
But it, as object most pursued, brings most
The woe upon the rearmost in the strife—
What need, I ask, what need that human aim
Should be so intertwined with human woe?
Is it a purpose or necessity
Or careless ordering in the source of law,
Or chaos, where the movement of the wreck
Which fills it, is the last that order felt
When order dying gave to chaos birth ?'

And here he paused. And then the Priest once more—
"'T is true indeed' responded, 'that distress
And pain and deprivation are the spur
By which the race of man is roused to climb
The difficult path of progress through the mist,
When emulation also lights the way.
But true it is that these have also laid
Effort—and oft—in weary, hopeless death.

'And true that all the lengthy history seems,
As by some strange necessity, instinct
With what to us appears as useless woe.

'But can this point to other than the hope
Of some new life which gives fulfilment's chance,
Of some new soil in which the seed, renewed,
Of human hope and toil may start again
With chance to gain development denied
In this condition, which as embryo
Serves to bring forth what tendencies the needs
Of that hereafter seek with high demand?

'If pain and toil and risk of limb and death
Attend to ban all schemes of human thought,
If even the skill of Medicine while it seeks
To stem the current of disease helps on
The inevitable misery, and saves
The weaker life to hand its weakness down

As guerdon to its child, what use is all—
If that alone which here is seen is all?

'The soul of Medicine aims I know to tear
The clinging roots of virus and disease
From out their seat in the thick soil of man :
'T is but a noble dream that hath not crossed
The mystic bound which parts the world of dream
From fact and life.   And granted that it cross
And stand amid fulfilments of the years
Of far-off time—what solace for the throng
Whose lot fills up the interval with woe?

'And how if even fulfilment of the dream
Assures not earth effacement of her woe ?
But shadows forth a struggle, life to life,
A fiercer slaughter than disease led on,
Without the hallowed pulse of pity's heart
To soften down its woe.   Efface Belief :—
The far result is but the crowded earth
Fashioned to one vast city, passion-filled,
And thick with that which is the direst curse
Of cities, cast upon their weakest hordes,
A lifeless life like dusk that has no sun
Nor evening star nor hue nor glow, nor gives
A promise forth of even the moon of night ;
But blanks and blacks unto the utter dark :
And men in useless struggle for the aim

Of equal space and equal share and chance,
Bent to the sensual, blind to scope of Faith,
Dragged through the struggle by their chosen chiefs,
And skulking in the ruined earth as thralls
Of some few tyrannies, that hold for rein
And bit each new design and artifice
Twisted from Science and from natural lore
As instruments of multitudinous death
Or multitudinous torture—   So I dream
The fair Elysium of a crowded earth
Torn from all faith in all but what it sees.

' But if some Power could sudden from the crowd
In days which are to us not dream but fact
Weed those whose idle blood or thriftless hearts
Bring sequel unto friend and kin, of want,
And all whose dust-dry hearts know only self
For purpose of existence, and look down
With careless eyes upon the pangs that stood
As steps by which they mounted unto ease
And silken sloth ; and all whose thoughts deceit
Has formed to tentacles of hideous fraud ;
And all the vice whose aim lies o'er a path
Of hearts downtrodden to poisonous mud of shame ;
There still remains one cloud to pour its woe
Upon the sunlit soil of such a scene :
Mistake brings suffering oft as deep as crime,
And hearts that have love's weakness, not its strength,

Nurse seeds of vice to breed new crop of wrong,
Nor is there an uprooting of the tares
Without therewith uprooting of the corn.

'Then is the prospect dark and nought but dark?
It seemed not so to Him whose faith supreme
Sought, through that supreme suffering of the Cross,
The solving of the mystery of pain.

'Therein He held for Faith a steady lamp,
Where all earth's best before had only held
A flickering flame, that showed but could not light
The deep whereon their eager hearts were led
By impulse irresistible to embark
To seek the solving of the mystery.

'And even grant that earth in days to be
Might be Elysium, and the far-off throng
Reap harvest of a woeless tide of joy,
The harvest won by generations gone,
Through tears and blood and suffering, for that hour
And them who on their distant sires in scorn
Will turn their eyes, or pity, or with feet
Tread thoughtless down their dust and seek no name,
Nor spend a solitary regretful sigh
Upon the mighty epitaph writ large
Over the tomb of generations past,
"These lived, these suffered, and in nameless dust
Fulfilled their fate, for future men there-through

To gain the light for which themselves had died : "
What compensation for the toil that won
Such high result, except to share the prize?
What help but hope that there is plan beyond,
And this which present consciousness can grasp
And share is fragment only of the whole,
And the great whole is that of One who knows
And notes the needs and meed of every part
As deeply as He knows the general bent
And movement of the whole, a plan not less
But more a plan that it is vast.'
       'You seem,'
The man of Science here joined in, 'to say
Since life and pain are bound in breakless chains,
And life has sometimes immaturity
Of end, that some continuance of life
Is sequel; so through life and life you lead
Perhaps to immortality as bourne.
I might believe it too, more proof its voice
Sounding in unison, if men alone
Bore pain. But pain is attribute of life
In lowly forms as well as highest grade ;
You should extend your immortality
To all if it be granted unto some.
Or if not pain, but pain unjustly brought,
Is that stern deep in which you lay the rocks
Of your new world, or life too soon cut short,
Which seemed to merit or to need extent

Prolonged, is to receive such consequence,
Either you frame new meaning to "unjust,"
Or wreathe round immatureness such a cloud
As dims all certain traces of its shape,
Or where from man to monad down can end
Your line of claimants?   Where to monad down
The form which has not that same ground of claim?'

  'The claimants end, it seems to me,' replied
The Priest, 'where reason fails to give or grasp
The thought, at such a point as whatsoe'er
Of reason or of fancy is, knows naught,
Nor aught conceives of thought of other life,
Nor has the longing which begets the thought;
But where the concept takes within the mind
A shape, if in that mind is dower besides
Of choice between the wish that draws and will
That fences in ; of judgment that decides
For one as right against the other wrong :
In beings holding this as heritage
The instinct pointing onwards lives as part
Of thought that knows itself as thought, and will
That knows itself distinct from its resolves.
In these arises capability
Of newer pain, a pain pursuing will
That steels itself to face for principle
A fate of torture which it else could shun.

These surely claim some compensation more
Than that which is the due of simple pain.'

So in the maze of that dark mystery
Which girdles all the realm of life their thoughts
They led.   But eve had come, and with the eve
The clang that spoke the hostel's table spread.
And as the eve proceeded slowly grew
The increasing light, the silent clouds rolled back
Before the glowing calm, and left the heaven
And bared the glistening snows, yet here and there
In tender drapery hung.   As sculptor's hand
Lays bare the dream of limbs divine that rose
Before his thought, and wreaths the harmony
Of robe around the harmony of limb.

And high the inaccessible whiteness rose
Of those huge summits mounting up to heaven,
And seemed at once to hold themselves afar,
And in their clearness to have deigned approach,
Blending the sense of near and sense of far.

Then the sun sank behind the violet-dark
Of jagged peaks cut clear upon the light
Of pallid sky, and soon a misty shade
Hung blue around the downward throngs of firs
And clad the steel-grey rocks, and reached the foot

Of glacier clutching close the awful steep
And forced to brink of falling; then across
The verge of downmost snow.

                But far on high
The mountain tops in pureness looking forth
Unto the hues of heaven stood glory-wreathed
Ineffable in burnishing of gold,
And mingled rose and purple-softened shade;
As by reception of the ethereal glow
Rapt unto melting with internal fire
That lit without consuming.

                So themselves,
Above the chaos of the rocks that strewed
The tortured bosom of the darkening earth
They lifted, passing in seraphic thrill
Of light, like hope that sees a hidden sun,
Into the shadow of entombing night.

V

GRAPPLE WITH GRIEF

A YEAR ago the path to high success
Had seemed to Runimont his destined way,
But casting down her palms and turning short
Success disowned her path which sickness seized
And strewed it o'er with her encumbering thorns.

A year ago there was a face he saw
Which filled his heart with thrills of love, yet filled
With all the chillness of mysterious fear;
But out from under shade of fear crept hope,
And seemed to bring the sapphire into heaven,
And light the world with hallowed light of joy.

A year ago and hope just risen fell:
Words from the lips of Wake that swept his brain,
As when tornado fells the forest, fell
Upon his ears, and showed a passionate hope
Already formed in his companion's heart
That sought for love's fulfilment where his own

Had felt the longing for fulfilment rise.
But to his unsuspecting friend no sign
Gave Runimont, and spake no word to show
That in another heart than Wake's the love
Had risen whose loss would darken all his life.
Yet did the crashing tempest of his thoughts
At first wake thunders in his brain, and raise
Emotion's battling tumult in the heart,
That flashed the fury of its lightnings forth.
But out from all the clattering anguish spake
One thought with calm, and kept the calm of tone
Amid the multitude of hissing thoughts
That with excited din chased sleep away,
A thought which held forth friendly aid to lift
His heart from out the turmoil of the wreck :
Never should wish nor word of his nor deed
Effect the misery of his friend.   Resolve
As armour battle-proof encased the thought.

But even so Resolve may hold the heart
And bar the gate to its assailant foe
Until the hour which gains its longed for aim,
Yet in the very citadel itself
Bring on the famine which within works woe
And fevered rising of revolt.
                              And waste
Had laid on Runimont its heavy hand :
His cheek was paler still that heretofore

Was pale : his power of thought too soon each day
Was spent as fire that blazes out its life,
And toil, whose length not hours but minutes spanned,
Reached its exhaustion's limit all too soon.
And all the dreary tide of longer day
Lay leaden on the dragging of his path
Through desert that gave flowerless wide expanse
To answer to the sunless waste of cloud.

    Once more the friends had met.   The meeting place
And point of earliest halt an inn that stood
Above a river's bank, and from its height
Looked down upon the waves of green-grey flood
Rushing in foamy turbulence of path
Below the jubilant thunder of cascade.
Across the flood rose here and there a crag
By castle crowned, or group of pines, to raise
The dull monotony of vineyard-slope
To higher strain.
            Short halt was purposed here
To visit scenes thronged thick with old romance
And buildings in whose crumbling worn remains
Spoke echoes of their worn and crumbled past.
But Runimont, unequal to the day,
Unhappy if his weakness should debar
His friends from aught of interest or delight
Had stayed behind alone.
               And evening came,

F

And he to meet and welcome their return
Strolled slowly on the river's lofty bank
And gazed upon the impetuous rush below,
So glad and so victorious and so strong
In joy of bounding plenitude of life—
Wide contrast to the weary course of his—
He felt a wail within his heart that came
In wail of words and left his parted lips.

'Roll on, oh stream—thou hast at least a course—
A destined path.   And though thy pitiless banks
Hem thee and torture that thou ravest thus,
They cannot stay the victory of thy flow.
Thou bearest in that glorious rush as dust
The comminuted pride which once was rocks
Crowned adamantine on the mountain's height,
And spoiled by glacier-fountains slowly-stern,
And tossed unto thine issuing infancy
To bear afar or fling aside in scorn.
Thou stayest the encroaching of the plundering sea,
Meeting it with those spoils from mountains torn.
Thou hast a destined course, oh happy stream !
Happy to have a fate whose struggles hew
Its ample path.   My heart lies like a waste
Of stone and reed and willow channelled thick
With aimless wanderings of uncertain flow,
That now lie dry of thought, and now fill up
With waves of gurgling woe—but have no aim.

O for the triumph of a rushing flood
To sweep the stone-strewn level of its thoughts,
And give to its meandering misery
A destiny of hope whose torrent strength
Rolls down the impetuous foam of victory.
O happy stream !
            What lies upon the foam
Like dull red glow of fire, and steals aslant
The rocks ? And on the dusky green of trees
It lays its tinge. 'T is thou, departing Sun !
Art thou but anguished light that thou dost send
On wave and rock and tree a hue that seems
The hue of pain ? The storm-throes rending deep
Thy bosom which incessant quiver holds
And fiery qualm . . . wouldst thou they fling their light
To stain, but not to glad the thing it meets ?

' Lo where the quivering orb nears like a bark
The level shore of far horizon-rim,
The massy clouds aglow, the sky aglow
With that red pain. . . . And now the shore is near—
Is nearer . . . close . . . and the red hero writhes
In Nessus garment which distorts his shape
And bows his form that doubles on itself
Rolled up in anguish—and he sinks as one
Who gasps in death !
            And, even sunk, he weaves
O'er the pale sky such dreams of gorgeous hue

On cloud and spreading mist, as follow him
Like the high thoughts and memories which thrill
The breast of sorrow weeping noble death.

' How envious round the glory of that light
Creep up yon clouds and crowd, invidious-dull,
To sweep the memories of its glow away,
Forerunners these of vengeful night.   O night,
Vengeful but vengeful sad that veilest earth
In dream — the dream of one whose thoughts brood dark
Upon the past, wast thou not, night, for rest ?
Bring rest, not dread, then ; quiet, not distress
Of fevered brain, bring dream that is not fierce
With lightning throes, bring slumber that may lull
And linger—not the startling of a crash
Clamouring like ruin almost as the hand
Of sleep lays touch to soothe that whirl of pain—
The rush of thoughts that light the brain with fire.'

The near approach and voices of his friends
Made then soliloquy to cease, and soon
Was either arm in friendly hold received,
And in the tenderness that gives the grasp
A softness which betokens strength was kept.
And voices shaded with a love reserved
Yet deep told over all the day's events.

VI

THE SERAPH-CALL

THAT eve they sat around the Priest, and begged
Rehearsal of some tale to pass the hour
. While eve was darkening to the deep of night.

Awhile he pondered, then he thus began :

'The roll of waters rising in low wave,
And glancing in the grey clear light of eve,
Crept on the shore with long low rumble, calm,
Repeated, deep.   And in that saddened roll
So full, so muffled, swelling speaks a voice
As of a mighty sorrow borne not quelled
But borne—so long, so well, so patient borne
It seems to roll its sympathy to soothe
The heart impatient at its spur of grief.

'And near the rolling tide a maiden sat
Not listening to its voice, yet hearing all
As distant rumble on the shore of thought.

For in her heart was wail and bitter grief,
And on her lips were words of wailing pain.

'" He kissed me.   'T was but meeting of the lips
For his heart came not with the kiss—his heart
I know was with another and his thought
Pictured another's face before his face.
Felt other lips approach his lips—not mine—
His heart was with another—not with me—
And when my eyes looked into his I saw
Beneath their hueless veil the distant gaze
Of thought adream—afar from all of me.

'" How could his heart be false—be false and turn
The coldness of its thoughts drained bare of love
On me who gave him never cause for change?
That limpet clings with stedfast trustfulness,
And neither gentle wave with wooing voice
Nor surging tempest can unfix its trust,
Nor aught but death, and thus my heart on thee—
On thee my rock—if only to itself
That rock be true, its limpet-hold would keep.

'" O love, my heart is full—is full of thee,
But in it, like the wintry cry of wave,
A moan is asking, 'Canst thou, couldst thou change?'

'" O but what lying thing art thou, my tongue,

That speakest thus of falseness and of change?
What prompted thee, my heart, to give my tongue
Rein to betray in word suspicion's thought?
Canst thou suspect, yet deem that thou art true?
Yet criest thou thus because thou holdest true!
My heart is true, my heart is love alone,
And yet it shivers through and through with doubt."

'Thus doubt, and anger at the very doubt,
And fear, and love that rising with a scourge
Smote and drove forth the fear, and doubt, then sunk
To bitter wail, in turn held up the lash
To scourge her heart. She sate beside the tide
That rumbling clambered up the sounding shore,
But short way from her home. The hour was past
Unto whose stroke no lover's footfall gave
The answer of appointment kept, long since
Was past, and first her heart unto itself
Had feigned such reason and excuse as love
Could seek to give a meaning to delay,
Then other and then other, till the stream
Recurred in useless and repeated flow.
Then came slow blank, and then remembered change
Of voice and mien that late seemed his she loved.
And doubt and torture drove her to the shore
To pace beside the waves with restless feet ;
Then to sink weary gazing towards the deep.

'And still he came not.

Then at length, by tread
Of steps approaching roused, she turned and saw
Her sister near, and at her sister's side
One she scarce knew, and only knew as friend
Of him who had not come.

In act to turn
She caught too soon their looks before disguise
Could mask them.   He as from her lover brought
Excuse of absence, but she heard the note
Which told the lips were conscious that they spoke
A foreign tongue of unaccustomed sound,
And spurned the words that left them as they spake.

'And then through pointed question, and reply
Which sympathy and sorrow veiled in part,
She drew the tale of wrong that turned her doubt
To fiercest certainty.   The man was false,
Was false, was traitor, and was hers no more!

' Her form rose towering o'er its wont, in scorn
That flung the indignation from her eyes
In rapid flash, and then from rigid height
To limpness sank.   She uttered forth a cry,
Long moaning like the moaning of the wave
That crept towards her feet, and strove to give
Its limpid kiss.   Then suddenly she turned
And trode as one who felt the ground she trode

Strewn o'er with villanies of human thought,
For foot of high disdain to trample down,
And spake no word, but in that speechless scorn
Entered her home, and straight within her room
Enclosed, in dark and silence passed the hours,
Entreaty-deaf, until her fevered brain
Poured forth its train of phantoms, and drove wild
Its raving thoughts upon her shrieking tongue.

'And, when a moon had passed, a shadow pale
In weakness tottered from that room, to give
One weary promise of recovering strength,
Then in her sister's clasp of fondness died,
Who last survived, but broken and alone,
The loved ones she had nursed on beds of death.

'But he who had accompanied her steps
When pity bade him feign excuse for one
Who made not even excuse for broken vow;
And shared her sorrow for her sister dead
Found love for her alight within his heart.
But veneration trimmed the lamp of love,
And, though it fed and kept the flame aglow,
It fenced its burning unto steadiest light.
Nor would he enter on the sacred ground
Of grief too soon, till time had somewhat worn
Its barrier, and made open way within.
And then with reverent step his love pressed on,

And found reward for worship offered long,
That brought fulfilling of the altar vow
In noble bliss and loving duty shown,
And high example and incentive given
To those whose hearts with love increased the bliss,
A maiden and a boy—these two, and life
Was to their parents as a dream of joy
At ten years' end fulfilling still its course.

  '"Twas night, and through the spray and mist and cloud
Hung low to trail the climbing foam shot up
Fire-pinioned signals of distress at sea. . . .

  'Darkness and fury of the unseen sea,
And dim white tracks that crawl the yawning black
Which booms in thunder on the trembling shore—
Who calls for help across the raging dark ?

  'Who calls ? What matter who ? The call is there . . .
And hearts obeyed the call. Two hours of black,
Night's deepest, gone, slow glimmerings filtered through
Where clouds hung heavy o'er the hidden rise
Of moon that dimly showed the moving deep.
Twice on the crash and thunder of the foam
The lifeboat, launched, was sideways flung ; thrown o'er
The second time upon the shore, it crushed
The lives of two who manned. And then once more
Righted for effort new it waited those
Whose hands should take the oars the dead had held

'Brave hearts were round, but certain seemed the end,
And useless death as sequel of attempt
Even in the very act of starting foiled.

'Another signal rose athwart the cloud,
And sicklied o'er the glimmering shore with light
That seemed beseeching to keep unrevealed
The unready limbs and faces of the throng.

'The two stood watching on the midnight shore.
Upon her husband's arm her wifely love
Leaned close—but wordless as to lip her heart
Was crying unto him whose heart replied
In silent answer stronger far than word.

'"*I* bid thee *go?*   How can I bid thee go?
I keep thee *back?*   How can I keep thee back?
In every call from man a woman calls,
And voice of sister, mother, child, or wife,
And voice of these to *man* sends forth its call."

'A moment, and in answer to her thoughts
About her neck her husband's arms were flung,
And lips unvoiced on lips unvoiced impressed
A lingering kiss—the voice that dared not say
"Farewell" choked in their choking throats.   She felt
His parting steps.   She saw him climb and take
A vacant oar.   She heard the cheer which spake
Even through the howl of storm.   And then she saw

A shadow take the one remaining oar,
Then heard another cheer.
　　　　　　　　The slow bulk moved
And crawled awhile, and then was mixed with foam,
And with the foam was leaping on the waves,
And this time, victor of the surging surf,
The boat pursued its way.　This time seemed hope
To answer need.　But when the rocking dark
Of what they strove to reach was near, a cry
Howled piercing on the howling wind.　And less
The black thing grew, and less, and disappeared,
And wreck in fragments boiled upon the surge.

'What thing was that upon the lifeboat's prow
Rolled thumping?　Spar and form of man thereon?
They dragged the form from out the tempest's foam
Across the bulwarks.　Then again looked forth,
But watching long saw nought but barren surf,
And nought could hear but storm which fiercer grew,
Till howl of squall and dark of rushing rain
Swept wildly down and shorewards drove the boat—
No hope to rescue more, and strength o'ertaxed
Seemed scarce sufficient to secure return,
And in a pause of squall they turned the prow
Homewards for shore.　But storm again renewed
When shore was close its passion, and the coil
Of wave, almost in sight of her who watched,
Wrapped round the oar her husband held and flung

The haft about his face. He strove to seize
Its random-tossing shaft that smote and dashed
Upon the bulwarks him who strove, and broke
His arm, and when the boat just after thumped
The strand and sideways swung and then was heaped
Upon the surf aside, he, flung forth, fell,
And, on the rock his head struck, moveless lay.—
From out the creeping foam they dragged him dead.
And she whose anguished eyes beheld the corse
Lifted her eyes from that dead face, as men
Began to bear him homewards—and she saw
The face of him whose rescue was to her
Such cost. It was the traitor's face she saw.

'Alone and dreary—dreary and alone !—
The day the dimness of a long eclipse :
The night the shimmering of continual dream,
The morrow, length and dearth, and dearth and length
Whose far-off end leads but to other dream
And other morrow's length and dearth and length—
What shudder comes with thought of far-off days
And far-off months, and that eventless far
Which lies beyond the end of many months,
And length and dearth, and length and dearth through all !
No light of joy illumes that distant rim,
There is no beacon to such sea but death,
The lightless hope which stands to mark the shore,
And take into the dimness of the dark

That which but now was unto those behind
A visible life—and now is memory's dream.

'Alone and dreary—dreary and alone !—
Yet in the dark of thought arose a light
Like the waned moon which leads the coming dawn,
But rose as if behind embanking cloud.—
Alone and dreary, yet not all alone.
The twain, the treasures of the dead and hers
Still left.   In them again the dead arose
As living still.   In them came back the light
And—brought to winter day in them—the weeks
Began to rise from slow monotony
To varying note.   In them the months and years
Clothed their flat wastes with varied scene and hue.

' But ever seemed to her the rushing sea
To fill with wails and voices of the dead.
And night when scarce a breath disturbed the air
Even listening calm to ocean's slumberous roar
Seemed ever on the point to rise in howls
And lash the sea and slay the dead anew.

' She left the taunting coast to seek abode
Away from sea and wave and shore and tide,
That never more the night with horrid voice,
And cold wet shingle clattering to the wave,
Bring back the hour of horror and the death.

'And with return of power to brain and life
Her heart sought ease in solace of distress
As one who thus with kneeling wish besought
Cessation of the grief of grieving hearts,
And when she could not beg release poured forth
The fulness of a passionate sympathy,
That sought for pardon for the prayer which failed.

'And as maturity of growth produced
In the memorials of her husband's past
The upright carriage of his noble thoughts,
And chivalrous pride of self-devoting deed,
And brought reminders of the buried lips
In voice that spoke the same melodious love,
Life seemed once more to catch its morning light,
And upwards mount in forenoon's growing glow,
And peace to fill the wind that soothed the flowers
And win the fragrance they with longing poured;
And even when, summer gone, the autumn sky
Crowded its glories round the setting sun,
The autumn leaves with blossoming of death
Refulgent spoke a voice which, though not hope's,
Seemed to fall on the silence of her heart
Like echo from a voice that once was hope's
Uttered afar and in the past, but now
An echo only, speaking from that past.

' Night came, not noon, upon that morning peace.

'An arrow's flight from where she dwelt event
Had brought the man whose face recalled the past,
Nor had a month upon his nearness lapsed
When wrapped in gleaming tongues of rising flame
His home made night red mock of day, and cry
Rose round and up of "fire," that shakes the limbs
Of those it wakes from sleep with sudden fear.

' Her son had heard the shout and woke and saw
Faces of anguish in the upper rooms
That gazed through casements if below appeared
Help from the awful death.
                          He hasty threw
His clothes about his limbs and rushing forth
Met by her room the mother he adored.

' "Must you go too ? "   A moment welling up
Her woman's anguish swept before its strength
The sober judgment of her soul.   Her son
With widened eyes of wonder took the words,
Astonished at the emotion new and strange ;
But while he gazed the sudden storm was o'er.
She bade him go and do his father's deed,
That was his father's child in noble thought,
And breathed a blessing with her parting kiss :
Then turned, and in her room on bended knee
Fell down.   And tears of anguish weltered hot
Between the trembling fingers placed to hide

Her torturing shame before her present God ;—
He then had deigned, from His supremest throne,
The exaltation of a seraph touch
Kindling forgiveness and the thrill of help
And benison of an injurer in his need.—
And she, with self's unready bars had met
The coming of that holiest messenger !

' Her anguish rained its flood within her heart
Upon her prostrate thoughts that dared not rise
And ask forgiveness, nor even prostrate dared
To kiss the sacred footprints of her Lord.

' But the young heart went forth, the danger thrill
Rousing his daring purposes.   And thrice
His courage rescued from the smoke and flame
Their shrieking spoil.   He entered for a fourth,
The last remaining life to snatch from death,
But they who saw him cross the fence of flame
Saw one who passed in sacrifice to God.

' They faltered out unto the mother's ear
The tale, and saw the gleam of pride flash forth
A moment from her eye, then dull itself
Unto the lead of swoon.   Delirium's dream
Of fire and shriek of her who felt her son

Aflame was swoon's awaking, day and day,
Wasting her till her life was all but gone.
But life groped back its way and brought its mate
Reason to hold awhile its throne.

                          Not long
She waited for the triumph-car of pain,
Her call for high translation unto rest.'

VII.

DUTY'S DEMAND FOR VICTIMS

THEN ceased the voice of him that told the tale,
And they who listened sat with silent lips,
Till soon the hour for slumber coming near
Drew to their several chambers all the group.

And sweet was night with its soft balm of wind
Moving and sinking back to rest, as waked
Awhile from dream, then passing back to dream,
And its high moon watching like pallid nurse
With hopeful smile the sufferer's transient sleep,
Her tranquil light lit up the feathery foam
And rolling wave, and gemmed the dews of pines,
And shimmered o'er the far horizon's peaks,
And dreamed amidst the mists that here and there
Rose o'er the stream like spectral floating forms.
Such night as in the memory lives and brings
When even the course of rolling years is gone
A fragment of its peace.
                    For Runimont

Not peace but restless stream of rushing thought
Filled all the midnight hours, till glint of dawn
Was now not far to come.   He rose and left
His useless couch, and through the casement peered
Upon the sleeping scene.   The moon was low,
And long the shadows.   Night was dreaming down
Itself in utter calm that seemed to taunt
The restless anguish of his fevered brain,
And on the window-pane his low voice moaned.

'They were too sweet—but yet I would not rouse
Those lost dead hours again.   But nevermore
To me can come the thrills of such a joy,
Nor evermore the stillness of such rest;
But like the vanished sun they leave behind
A spectre of themselves, to haunt the night
With pallid glow that deepens into black
The thronging shadows.   Night of night it sinks
With darkness, not with rest, upon my heart.

'Why were we made to bear this load of woe?
And what avail, from night to night, to bear
The fever of this fire—and no relief,
But ever torture newly garbed comes forth,
Or newly weaponed with some scourge to smite?
If it were only pain, I know wherewith
To meet the pain, if but this ceaseless rush
Of driven thought like hound lash-stung to speed

Would stay its furious course.

                    Dost thou so haste,
O setting moon, to sink below the earth
And leave the scene to helpless utter dark
Too deep for shadows, and the shuddering night
To silence, not to peace? Is that the end?
And is that end a parable of death—
Silence not peace?

                    What cause why thoughts so oft,
Regard it as the first of things to shun,
And yet regard it as a tempting sleep?
If death be rest, why should we dread repose?
If pain in other guise, why seek that pain?

'Rest and no hope beyond . . . the wakeless sleep
Of all of faculty . . . of feeling . . . thought . . .
Of all that could be conscious . . . even this
Creeps like a shudder . . . not a thrill of peace.

'If death ends all what purpose in the web—
And meaning—of the life of men? Distress,
Evil, and pain, lit up by golden threads,
Weaved in, of hope! If only here that gold
Is ours 't is tawdry tinsel that soon blacks,
And all the threads lose hue, and there remains
Only the web, dull, useless for its aim.
Life calls for joy—response unto the call
Is pain. Life prays its prayer for aim fulfilled:

Response unto the prayer is aim's defeat;
And yet through all a voice imperative
Requires through these incentments goodness reached
As death-wound earned in struggle, and sends thrills
As if from fever of diviner life,
Of self-devotion that for sole reward
Receives its pulse of joy at doom.   And oft
Grow yearnings only deeper when repressed,
And the heart struggling with itself lives life
The keener for the struggle, and by act
Of burying love that would emblossom it
Roots it the more securely.   Still the voice
Demands the self-devotion, and the bar
Secured to fasten in the yearnings chained
Within their cell the heart, and then the grave
For sepulchre of love,—with voice so stern
Demands, as makes refusal to be cost
Of reverence that to self is due from self. . . .
The shrine of virtue stands from age to age,
And hearts are that which feeds its altar-fires,
Hearts into which the Priestess Duty thrusts
The knife to slay.   She claims the lofty-souled,
The best, as food for that high altar-flame,
But leaves the ignoble dust of selfish hearts
To work their will and make of life a feast ;
And pomp and vanity and slanderous tongue
Of faction heap their tinsel on their names,
And scribe such epitaphs upon their tombs

As make the silence holier of the graves
Of those who for the sake of duty died
In secret—in that secret whence the voice
Of prayer goes upward to its secret God . . .
Yes holier, though the graves hold nameless dust
For path of those that tread, but know it not,
Therein the lost remains of lofty life.

'Yet on the pale face of the broken in heart
I have beheld a glory that surpassed
Even beauty's self, a chaster radiance lit
When hope—despair re-risen—sad hope that dreams
Of life to be has touched with wand that heart,
And spoken of more than death beyond the bourne
Of death, and stirred its impulses to strive
To higher than themselves.
                                 Can it be dream,
A dream with which God mocks the hearts of men?
And has He formed them thus to feign and build
Ideal forms of loveliness and thoughts
Wherewith His passionless gaze should feast itself,
And take no heed of all the writhing shapes
Which build and perish in the fateful toil,
Except to taunt them by a lying gift
Of hope to soothe the weariness of woe
In the death-struggle with their misery,—
Deluding them therewith to mortal pain?

'It cannot be !   I know not what forbids,
But there is *that* which bars and bans the thought,
And speaking in the heart it reasons thus :
That what to man has seemed, in spite of men,
The highest and the noblest of their deeds,
And loftiest of their thoughts is, in itself,
The mortal copy of immortal form,
A poor a feeble rudiment and sign
Of some completeness, some perfection held
As soul of soul in Him who leads there-through
The onward march of man.   The True in us
Is in no lesser sense the True in Him ;
And uprightness for sake of which He bids,
Through instinct, man to follow path of pain
Is part of Him.   Truth His, and uprightness,
How should the Upright and the True delude ?'

VIII.

THE PROBLEM OF DESPAIR

THE morrow from the cataract and stream
They took their way, and reached a hostel throned
Crag-high above the floor of emerald lake
That slept far down beneath its mountainous guard.
And from the hostel over ridge and gap
Of rock-walled valley stretched the view to heights
Whose distance blended white of snow and tinge
Of glacier green to pallid grey.   And close
Were Alpine pastures mown for autumn swathe
And, down below, the green of clustered fir
Spire-pointed in their myriad tips that rise
With heavenward aspiration ever true.

A love like woman's love, and tenderness
Like woman's thought held Runimont and Wake.
A bond, the strongest of the bonds that held
The band of friends, where every bond was strong.
Companioned years and interchange of thought
And search together into problems veiled

In mystery had opened heart to heart,
And added unto this in Runimont
The fire of self-renouncing love leapt up
In fulness that consumes with rapid glow
The heart in which it lives, and thus his love
Had wrapped his friend in arms which all their length
Put forth their ivy-strength of clasping roots ;
And Wake with all the fondness of regret
Beheld the sickness-waste which paled his friend
And fevered all his thought, and seemed to point
Unto an hour of parting, whose mere hint
Brought shudder through him, and his love the more
Clung unto what in accents so distinct
Seemed to be speaking of departure soon.

'Twas morn of gentle air and tranquil sky
Blue in the deep-hued intervals of clouds,
That when at times they hid the glowing sun,
Took at their rim the light and poured it forth,
And let the gentle trailing of their shade
Cross the far snow.   And where the shadows left
The snow, it beamed as with the smile that lights
The grateful face of one receiving joy.

And Runimont contemplating the scene—
Not from the hostel far—upon a rock
Was seated.   Further strolling on his friends
Had wandered.   He, his brush in hand, essayed

To limn some thought of that whereon he gazed,
And shadow out impression of the form
And hue and light. But vain had seemed attempt.
His feeble brush was drag unto the wheel
Of his impetuous thought. At length annoyed,
He laid it down. The mountain tops had signed
Unto the wandering clouds to clothe their snow
With stoles that here and there hung heavy o'er,
And heavier o'er the heaven the cloud-groups hung.

His thought, set free from stroke of hand and brush,
Made of the mountain height and cloud her path
To other height and other cloud and steep.

'The hold of Truth, oh Christ, in massive clouds
Lies like an Alp embanked, and on its peak
Men's thoughts borne rolling through long centuries
By aspiration's storm or wail of woe
Themselves have flung, but its stern strength stands up
Impenetrate, and keeps them drawn around
And wreathed in its attraction close ; and they,
Turned into tears by its impassive cold
And icy touch, roll round and round and fall
In weariness upon its foot, thrust back
To whence they rose to rise with effort new,
And with their ineffectual wings to strive
And lift themselves towards the Zenith height.
But, far above, the empyrean spreads,

That infinite-far which Truth's stern height regards
Awful and vast and blank . . . unreachable.
And Thou hast part in all the destiny
And thought of man, oh Christ, and comest with hope
Upon the wilderness that gave no track,
But closed the searcher in its deadly sand.

   'Yet rises dread at sight of Thee that fronts
The hope whose face smiles sweetly at Thy side.

   'What if Thy teaching of the life to be
Came like a bleeding sweat forced out by pain
At seeing life's injustice and its wrong?
What if the love-strong throbbings of Thy heart—
Its justice and its pity—gave the thought
As of despair, and if bewilderment
Of yearning, clutching at the heart and mind,
Gave such intensity to hope as brought
The concept forth—so sadness and despair
Aroused the extasy to living blaze
As lightning from the midnight cloud of doubt?

   'Yet grant it. What has Reason that denies
Perception of the truth to pain, to love,
To pity, and to justice and despair?
That these should have no hands by which to find
Its rocks, which in the utter dark that blinds
The Reason, hold them ready to the grasp

Of the worn swimmer in the swirling stream?
And so Thy dower of these, divinely great,
Found and revealed the Truths divinely true?'

The morning passed, him musing, noon was near,
And his eye fell on his unfinished sketch
And idle brush. They imaged out his thoughts
And even his life. The hues were there—the tools—
But faltering where its sweep should limn with power
The hand that held, and feeble, where its stroke
Should give the final touch of light and life.

Wake's voice in foremost leading of his friends
Recalled his thoughts from dream. The sketch that lay
Beside him idly, brought applause from all—
Even incomplete. But on the weary face,
So lost in sad reflection, read the Priest
Suggestion of the thoughts whose impress lay
Thereon and veiled it, as the moon the sleep
Of billows when thin clouds enfold her face.

''Tis failure and is incomplete, you say,
And incomplete it is'—so spake the Priest.
'Yet here I see the distance-softened peak
And ghostly light that rims the upmost line
Of summit-crowning snow where, curling o'er,
It overhangs its throne of precipice,
And gazes down upon the sea of ice.

And smiles, receiving from that icy breast
The sunlight thoughts of its tumultuous joy ;
And here are clouds that at command of wind
Move delicately-hung in mellow air,
And shadows sleeping under rocks that jut
And take the light.   And here are trees that seem
In act to take suggestions of the breeze ;—
Though incomplete the half, when such, is more
Than many wholes.   And even thus the life,
Which seems to human eyes to reach no aim,
Nor gain reward but failure, may be more
Than life which seems to gain its destiny.—
If it be true to its high aim of Truth,
That life shows forth the Master's outline limned
With strength and power, while others, side by side
With that, are feeble strokes of lesser men.'   ·

And Runimont with eye but not with lip
Gave answer.   For his eye was turned to gaze
Upon the speaker's face as if it saw
Some near approach of strand before concealed.

IX

LEPROSY AND LOVE

UPON the rock again in afternoon
 They sat and looked upon the gorge below,
That widened from far distance, in the front,
In blue of shadows cast by roofing cloud
Which now but here and there gave gap for light.
A little time and one long beam of sun
Lit up a hill that in the gorge's depths
Stood chapleted with ruin, that it gleamed
Pictured upon the shadowy scene beyond,—
A living present on a past, part dim
And part effaced.   Even in the distance clear
The ruin stood as ruin, not as rock,
Or doubtful whether of the twain it were.

'A legend,' said the Priest, 'of elder time
That ruin owns.   A haughty race and fierce,
The race that held it, driven to this retreat
By foreign sword, which in the lower vales,
Together with the harvest of the soil,

Reaped harvest of the hearts which owned the tilth.
But round their lord the remnant drew and made
Of yonder crag the hold, from which in day
Of curtained cloud and dark of night they swept
Through gorge and forest on their foe, and snatched
From under the remorseless stranger's hand
Sister and orphaned child and wife, made slaves,
Grief-silent, on the hearths that unto them
Were full with memories of sweet love and home.
And round yon hold they built new homes, and sowed
New slopes of grain, and crowned the craggy steep
With castle walls, and did their lord's behest,
And held him as their sire and were as sons.

' Rude festival to greet the finished toil
Of rude abode was over.   On the hearth
The log-fire died : the rocky dwellings round
Were silent in the stillness of the night.
The castle's mistress on her pallet lay,
No couch of ease, beneath the stony vault
Strewn on the bareness of the stony floor ;
And to their close the months were drawing near
Of bearing that sweet burden which is hope.
Sleep first kept far—then hovered near, then fled,
As taunting her who sought its proffered boon,
Until her thoughts to paths unwonted turned :—
The time to be, the fate of that new home
And those who owned the fastness.   Men, that day,

Had greeted its completion as defence
Of them and theirs, defenceless else. Her lord
Asleep beside her, thought of pride to all. . . .
Would rampart of defence be sometime changed
To tyrant's keep? And that which should of her
Be born be in the far-off years the curse
And not the boon of hearts, and blessing change
To iron-throated hate, and hail the fall
Of walls round which the new rejoicing song
That day and eve had wandered up?

         'Twas thus
She mused and dreamed. And then her thoughts, too clear,
From dreamy turned to wakeful, kept wide-eyed
Her hours of rest, till, weary grown, she sank
In longer spell of slumber. Then half-waked
She saw the narrow ray of moonlight, fenced
By casement, streaming through the room. A shape
Was in the pallid ray, whose garments seemed
As floating on the fluttering light, and hair
Enwreathing like a floating cloud its neck
And heaving breast. And voice in murmur, first,
With far off tone and meaning dark she heard
Repeating and repeating some refrain,
Which when she grew more wakeful clearer spake,
And told that when for justice love of power
Should own that dwelling, then Gehazi's bane
Would end the race, and ruin lay its hand
For ever on the castle's empty walls.

H

' Dread roused her unto fullest wakefulness :
She started up and sat.   No form was there,
And nought but moonlight moving on the mist,
That through the casement's gap had wandered in.
She rose, and looking through its opening saw
A silver sea of moving mist, whose waves
Just reached the aperture and cast their crests
Into the gap, to spread them in the room—
A sea of shapes without her fancy saw,
Of spirits moving clad in white, and one,
She thought, had come within to speak her dream ;
And, high above, the moonlight lit the lines
Of glimmering glacier-billows, and her thoughts
Traced there a long array of angel-throngs
Mounting in white a pathway up to heaven.

'Smile was the welcome that her lord bestowed,
Receiving from her lips at morn the tale—
No ghostly voice had vexed his heavy sleep—
Yet smile glassed over inner fear that rose
As if of warning given by spectral lips.

'The son next day was born to whom he left
His heritage of risk, who handed on
To after-generations of his race
The legend of the warning, which kept back
The pride of power in those whose power increased,
Until the sixth succeeded as the heir—

Sole child of parents who to early graves,
Before his youth had reached maturity,
Were borne.   And he grew on to uncontrolled,
Having no will by curb of which his heart
Might learn how proud obedience elevates.

'Battle and rocky climb in chase of bear
Or chamois, and the wolf-hunt—these his joy—
And forth from wife and child his heedless will
Dragged the reluctant, unreturning steps
Of many left in death, laid low in fight ;
Or prey of faintness when their strength o'erborne
Forsook them on the mountain's weary height;
Or left as mangled corse below the ledge
Scaled in precipitous chase.   But those he led
He made a terror to the land around ;
A band whose fierce endurance filled, with deeds
That startled, every lip and every ear,
And every heart with hate.   And envy rose
Among the powerful, snarling at his might.

'The daughter of a baron, power-enthroned,
Some distance off, on castled steep, awoke
New passion and imperious in his heart ;
At lordly group of tournament beheld.
And when refusal of the maiden's hand,
And scornful message from her father's lips,
Were answer to the burning of his love,

His tempest-rush upon the baron's home
Broke o'er the ramparts ere defence was formed,
Or warning given.   His cragsmen found a path
Into the very midst of noisy feast,
And left the hall the home of solitude,
Where in the horrid silence of decay
Retainer gazed his lifeless gaze on lord,
And lord on lady, and the mother held
Her stony clasp around her stony child,
And on the board the part-consumed remains
Of feast lay mouldering mid the staring dead.

'The maiden, carried to his mountain hold
And dumb at heart, in daze of sudden fear
And horror made his bride, one only child,
A maiden, bore, whose arms entwined and kiss
And love's young sweet caress brought back awhile
Like echoes, fragments as of something lost, -
The thrills of life and love.   But ere her years
Reached ten, the child to uncompanioned hours
And lonely thoughts was left, and moaned the loss
Of mother whom the kindred-riever death
Had snatched, and wandered o'er the embattled wall,
Or through the hall and dismal chambers, lost.

'And pity, like a dawn from out a dark
Which theretofore had never known a dawn,
Stole to the father's heart.   His thoughts began,

Regardful of the child, to follow her,
Then clung about her in continual hold ;
Then poured his torrent force of wilful heart
Its rushing strength on its new goal.   A love—
The she-bear's love—of savage parent strength
Consumed him.   Ever close beside him kept,
He taught his child to tread the dizzy ledge,
Taught her to tame the steed, and led her forth
Companion of his paths to join the hunt ;
And, save when need blew hoarsest, and the call
Warwards rang loudest out its trumpet-note,
Eschewed the impassioned longing of his past.

'Thus reached the maiden's years to womanhood,
The shapeling of her mother's high descent,
But dowered with somewhat of her father's will
And rugged love.
              But woe were his, whose hopes,
Unfavoured of the father, sought the child,
And made essay to win.   And yet the maid
Won worship and a reverence gained of few ;
But worship that unkneeling dared not show
Even the light movement of a whispered word.

'One, only, felt the baron's welcoming hand
Consenting stretched.   A man her father's peer
In somewhat of his savage wilfulness.
But him with scornful gaze, and lip that spoke

Repulsion and disdain, she heard.   Endowed
With instinct keen, and trained to keener still,
She pierced the thick disguise that wrapped his acts,
And through the mask which bore the guise of love
Saw the true face of heartless low desire.

'Guest often in the castle hall, and oft
Upon his daughter by her father urged,
She turned the more abhorrent from the thought
Of him and loathly clasp that flouted love.
And all the sullen efforts to compel
By which her father made the bitter days
Drag heavily, no entrance could compel
Within refusal's outposts.   From his guest
As hostess she with due acceptance took
The bidden dues from guest to host, and there
Her will raised up a fence of cold reserve,
Forbidding more approach.   Persuasion next
Which, like a tongue less natural than learnt
Was spoken, followed in her father's mouth
And, foiled, was changed to savage tongue of threats,
Whose loudness rang, as all things else, in vain.

'And vain besides was guard about her steps
In secret placed to note if otherwhere
Her love inclined.   For, orphaned of the care
And refuge of a mother's heart, her eye
Had learned to read the writing on the face

Of false and faithful. Warily and well
She searched before she trusted.
                        More there was
Which helped the maid. For in the peasants' huts
The motherless found many mothers' hearts
Where often want and pain had known her help,
And hearts of women there divining much
But silent, found the way to soothe their grief
For her, in watchful service secret shown.
And even within the castle's walls were those
Whose mask of true compliance, worn to stay
The baron's wrath and penalty, concealed
Devotion unto her and deeds of help.
And fear on her behalf in these discerned
Among their lord's retainers those in whom
Confiding were betrayal. They who watched
In watching guarded, giving secret sign
Which said beware, when danger seemed at hand ;
And, placed for overthrow, if there were he
To whom her heart was given, in faithful love
Were false unto the purpose of their watch.

'For unto them through means not all of her,
But yet of her in part, by step and step
The secret of her love became revealed,
And then device of willing hearts contrived
The meetings whose low whispered words of love
Made glad the long remainder of the hours,

And gave the strength to bear the long restraint
Of absence.   Even within the present ken
Of him her father chose and of himself,
Her father, moments passed whose secret signs,
Read only by the two, were eloquent
With comfort and the benison of love.
And times not few, the legend says, were those
Wherein discovery made so close approach
As all but trode the shadow of retreat.

'But jealousy has eyes on every rock,
And ears for every whisper even of air ;
And they who always on uncertain ledge
Of danger tread must sometime suffer fall.
There came an hour, at end of several moons,
In which the victim's steps were tracked, and word
Suspicion-winged, directed to the truth,
The baron's thoughts.   The note of warning came
From those who watched, of danger now supreme.

'Her lover, warned, assumed the palmer's cross,
Nor made delay : expedient fore-arranged
Between the lovers if event the need
Should bring ; hope faintly whispering that delay
And absence would perchance attain their end.

'And there was parting—meeting but to part—
Which pity and fidelity arranged,

And peril had no accents to forbid ;
The meeting of two shadows in the dark—
The grasping of a hand scarce seen, and lip
In voiceless pressure meeting lip that held
With stern repression even whisper back—
And after—leagues and sea and years that seemed
To widen out the time to measureless length,
Before those hands and lips should feel again
The joy of hallowing touch.
                         When distance gave
Security of life to him she loved,
The maiden sought to bend the baron's will ;
Revealing all the passion of her love,
And pleading with a voice and eagerness
That rang from wall to wall, and filled the room
With cry which seemed to clutch the very stones,
Yet found no entrance to her father's heart.

'Storm followed on the pleading, on his lip
Whitening, and in his thunder-shaded eye
Lighting a glare of fury. Stamping foot,
And fist tight-clenched, and roar of howling word,
Made quake the hearts of all within the walls
That, daring not to listen, heard. But hers
Felt bubblings of a wrath her will trode down,
That knew its strength and steeled itself to more.

'The pilgrim's path untraced, and not the cross

Of pilgrimage, was shelter from the wrath
That sought assuagement in the pilgrim's death.

'Nor came relenting even with lengthening time :
His wrath burnt on, but yet the maiden's will
Was not a metal easy to the flux
Nor leaf to ready shrivelling.   Siege he deemed
Long-placed would force surrender, but he feared
Lest forceful haste should tempt her, sudden stirred
By desperation, to the leap of death.

' But at the ending of a barren year,
That showed no sign of fruit to effort's toil,
The baron made from his high walk of wrath
Descent to plea.   More hard was plea to bear
Than even wrath.   But, changeless still, her face
In love's pale firmness spoke in unison
With what her lips responded.   " Unto him
My troth was given—to him my troth I keep."

'And then concealing from her that his plan
Was changed, her father's craft devised report
Spread by the lips of one whose steps approached
The fastness, as returning from the East,
That sore disease and lingering death had seized
Her lover, travel-worn in slow return.
And words of feigned farewell conveyed to her,
As if by promise made unto the dead,

Were hurled to wound her stedfastness ; and proof
Was forged in confirmation of his death.

'She stopped the passage to belief, and spurned
The words as false, and even overborne
With witness gave not way. " If he be dead,"
She said, " I am the more betrothed to him.
He died as mine, and *I* as his will die."

'One method more the father's anger tried
To force compliance. From her side he moved
Those whose long service had its secret tear
Of feeling for her grief, and all to whom
She might impart a word, and have reply
Of sympathy. And chain of close restraint
He placed about her.
     Then the maiden sank
And wasted in disease till, prostrate laid,
She stirred within her father's heart a fear
Which thrust awhile his mood of anger back,
And weeks of sickness tended by the hands
Of those his fear restored unto her aid,
Gave back her limbs to movement and to air :
But with the feebleness of ruined health.

'Her whilom power was gone, and with that power
The throne of calmness crumbled. Freedom given
Anew was ineffectual to its hope ;

It gave not back the vigour of the past,
And in a sort the baron gained his end.--
The maiden gave a cold assent to yield,
If tidings came not proving false the death,
And on the dearth of news a stated day
Should pass.

          Day rose to re-enkindle low
Hope that the day before had quenched, and quench
At night the hope it lit.   The morn prescribed
Came, and the flame of hope was ashen-cold.

‘And unadorned for bridal—for once more
The indignation which insouled her past
Raised high its front—she let herself be led
Unto the chapel’s dim-lit altar step
Listless, with thoughts unlistening and afar.

‘The priest’s sonorous voice began the rite,
That on her heart as on the chapel walls
Unmeaning fell.   But ere the vow was reached
That bound the bridal, there was at the door
A stir of the retainers, giving path
With murmurs to a leprous form that trode
Even to the entrance, where in fear they stood
Drawn back as from a spectral visitant.

‘The muffled movement caught the baron’s ear,
Who, turning, saw the leper.   As he gazed

Back came to memory what in burial hid
She long had kept—the legend long before
Told to his childhood's listening.   Panic-smitten
He paled as one who sees a sudden form
Which with its spectral fingers gives the sign
To follow to the mystery of death;
And, leaning on the arcaded wall, sank down
Upon the sounding floor whereon the clang
His armour made was requiem to his fall,
And stared his lightless stare of horror—dead!

' Meanwhile had sunk the utterance of the priest,
Who from the staring baron door-wards gazed,
And saw the living corpse of leper stand ;
And at the altar all, and even the maid,
Turned round in wonderment to know the cause.

'And by what instinct she her lover knew,
Disguised beneath that scale-white skeleton,
No tongue has told.   But while her father's corse
Was yielding unto its dead weight, her rush
Had reached the leper—round his neck her arms
She flung, and stilled his agitated lips,
That struggled to reveal how, smitten thus
With lingering death, he came to set her free
From vow to him, and found the gathered throng
Of bridal, and had sought unknown to gain
A glimpse once more of that long-worshipped face

To soothe, as dream of love, his closing days.—
She would not listen to the tale she knew
His moving lips were uttering ; but his hand
She took, and led him altarwards, and bade
The astonished priest, and with a voice and mien
Imperious even beyond her father's wont,
Repeat the rite to that white form and her.

'Wrath like a demon's staunchless vengeance filled
The baffled suitor, left without a word
To turn from vow and altar.   Ready armed,
His band of few retainers grasped, with him,
Their swords ; but, kept in check by steady gaze
Of greater numbers whom the open door
Showed swayed with a resolve o'ertowering theirs,
They curbed their present wrath to loose the rein
Of future vengeance.   And his muttered threats
The scorn of valour coldly took and smiled,
And bade him show completion of his words
In deeds that were less empty than were threats.

'And when upon the castle and their homes
He led attack—assault waked up to joy
Their olden battle-fervour.   Life and life
Went down before their weapons   but even so
The strife left battered walls and levelled homes
And waste of crops by flaming harvest reaped,
Before his death in blood made end to war.

'And she, regardless of the yielding walls
And missiles hailing round the castle's towers,
Filled hour and hour in binding up the wounds
Of men that bled with gladness, so her hand
But bound them.   And to child and woman, thronged
For shelter in the castle's court, she spoke
The words that stirred endurance in the heart
And soothing hope.   And every interval
Allowed by care of wounded men and sick
She gave to him on whom her wifely love
Poured all its pent devotion, sister-like,
In virgin nursing of his wasted form.
And while the life within that sepulchre
Dragged on its weakness, more devote, in scorn
Of superstition's fear she ministered
To all his need, and of her woe poured out
The wine of sympathy and help and joy
To sufferers who from out their pain to her
Looked up with awe and love.
                                        And when at length
The leper passed away she laid her down
In dim exhaustion's weary somnolence
In that same room wherein the spectral voice
Had given its ghostly warning.   Wasting there,
She died, but in the hour when death was nigh,
Beholding through the casement's aperture
The pallid rose of eve, which up the path
Of glacier-pinnacle spread its burnished glow,

Her eyes from languid somnolence woke up
Awhile to light, and something left her lips
That told of spirits rising glory-robed,
From woe, to mount the gleaming heights and tread
Their triumph-path unto the throne of God.

'No hand had touched the castle's battered walls
To heal their wounds.   But in the night which closed
Around the rite which laid her to her rest
Came storm in mountain fury, and its flash
And thunder-burst broke through the empty hall,
And rent the shivering walls.   And winds of night
Moaned ever through the gaps, and seemed a voice
That wailed in agony of blighted love ;
And fancy feigned a spectre wandering sad
Through all the haunted rooms ; and slow decay
Consumed the broken battlement and tower.'

X.

RUNIMONT'S VISION

D AY followed in the rear of day till came
The hour of further journeying. The Priest
And Runimont together took their way
In leisured travel, while the others clomb
The grandeur of the snowy slopes, and breathed
The mountain's upper air, and gazed, from crags
And summits fit for feet of gods, afar,
Over the low horizon of the world,
And ending crossed the crests, where far on high
The silent snow-seas slumber round the steeps
That o'er them, towering up in savage strength,
Stand black and scornful of the white assault
Of storm-driven snow, which in humility
Of drift they force to lie about their feet.

Weary the day that led to weary night,
And weary night that brought to weary day ;
Repeated and repeated, this his fate
Brought dread to Runimont, which dragged the length

I

Of weary day and wearier night to more :
Dread of a useless future, when the years
Should bear him on upon the changeful waves
Of fluctuating feebleness, till death
Brought ending to a life that left no trace
Even on the feeble waters where it passed.
And in the hours when darkest on the heart
Was laid the shadow of this fear, a wish
Crept through the shadow, seeking for a grave
That soon might close the hopelessness of life,
And came at times in wail of uttered word.

'Thy feet are slow, methinks Thy feet are slow,
The days drag on and weeks and trailing months,
And yet Thou com'st not with the word that bids
The struggler cease his struggling and lie down
In peace of rest.   At times, O Lord. when night
Rallied its stillness into storm, and winds,
Fierce shriekers, wandered through the startled air,
And lightning clove the shuddering tree and gave
Its thunder roar of triumph, has my heart
Thrilled with the thought " He comes perchance anon
By wind or lightning He will send His call."

'But yet no call.   Nor when I passed and paused
Beneath the mass which in the grip of cliffs
Hung, and the cliffs each moment wearier seemed
And ready to let fall the ready rock,

And thought was brightened into hope, that death
Might with a sudden burial put end
To the long labour,—neither then had hope
Thy mandate that it be at once fulfilled.'

Such thoughts at times swept o'er his mind, but gained
No hold, for Reason came with steady front
And claimed her sway and kept in manacle
The thought—unreasoning progeny of woe
And sickness—'Why endure and not make end?'

And sometimes in his weakest hours, when sleep
Hovered uncertainly about his brain,
His will, impaired and weary with attempt
To keep its hold upon itself, sank loose:
And dreams, confusing past and present, mixed
The things that were not with the things that were,
And brought unto his sight the face he loved.
One, o'er its comrades vivid, back and back
Came in his waking hours—her arms were stretched
A moment as in pain, that longed to clasp
Yet dared not, then asudden locked his breast
And held him in embrace, and on his neck
Her head sank soft, and shy love silently
Melted from shyness into happy rest.
And oft the face was lingering, and the kiss
Which only dream could ever know kissed on
When dream was over, and regret, with locks

Of aegis-bitterness, flung on the dream
A blighting stare which quelled its gaze of love.

And when awhile at times in slow attempt
Strength seemed to show return, his rousing will,
Like some old baron of the castled past,
Shook off the assailant dream and gave command
To close his memory's gates against the foe.

The Priest and Runimont the third eve reached
A wild ravine whose sides no stunted bush
Nor verdure held.   Such awful wall arose
Above the roaring stream whose thunderous fall
Dashed, down the narrow depths, from heights just seen
Far up in snowy distance, waves whose force
Smote almost with the shock of solidness ;
And even the air which their mad rush displaced
Swept like a roaring wind above their face.
Beyond the hostel rocks arose, as heaped
In bitter struggle's end of death.   Even these,
Except for stain of moss and lichen, held
No evident sign of life.
                        The night's wild horde
Of fancies rushed before the fevered brain
Of Runimont, and in fantastic dream
Rolled her he loved, beseeching, on the whirl
Of dashing torrent, and the solid wind
Rising therefrom beat back his vain attempt

To stretch his hand in wild desire to save—
And, gaping sudden to the storm of foam,
The path his rushing steps pursued in vain,
To follow and fling down himself to help,
Let down his steps to awful depth of fall
Wherein beyond his reach—nor more beyond
Than just to mock his touch—her hand was stretched,
And all the thunder of the awful deep
Spake ' Runimont' and ' Runimont' in voice
That was the utterance of her lips, and changed
To desolate toneless clamour, deafening ear
And brain, as in the boiling dark she sank,—
And he, dewed o'er with drops of anguish, woke.

Morn showed his face more pale, and trembling hands
More trembling, and his eyes red, listless, set . . .
Escape from scene so wild that gave no rest . . .
Escape, was all the wish he had within.

Up—upwards, fevered thought drove on his steps,
Up—upwards, for a glimpse of gentler scene
To calm with peace thought's horror.
                                                On they pressed :
The Priest with anxious and astonished heart
Companioning the pace he could not check.
The summit crossed, at eve they neared a spot
Where, o'er the rudeness of its slopes, the gorge
Had wrapped a garmenting of firs, festooned

In trailing grey of lichen, and the moss
Grew green about their feet, and lower down,
With sycamore and oak and chestnut green,
The valley's floor was widened out in stretch
Of grass that lay in evening's light of peace.

There in exhaustion's fever day by day—
Four days was laid the sufferer's prostrate form,
And then delay enforced for some return
Of strength detained the Priest and Runimont,
And from the fore-appointed meeting-place
Their friends came up the pass at message sent
To join them in their dwelling of delay.

And meanwhile grew the bond of confidence,
And brought its bud affection into flower
In him who nursed and him who suffering lay.

And of his past and his more inward thought
Spake Runimont unto the listening Priest,
And freely spake.   He told him how, while life
Was still the path of hope, and strength was still
His own, his voice was raised and heart to God
In prayer, whose sequel suffering followed close.

' I asked for suffering to arouse my will
To learn endurance, and for chastisement
To lift and to refine, but asked the strength

To toil withal, nor yield at scourge of pain,
But in that conquer. . . . After this my heart
Drew faltering back and shrank, and seemed to feel
That it had pressed too closely on its God.

'And then again the living ardour came,
And taunt of weakness smote me full, and stung,
And I once more crept close, and dared once more
To risk the prayer. And then 'twas scarce a moon
Had passed upon the uttering, and I knew
That He had girt me round with pain and made
Thought but the thrill of anguish.'
                                        Thus he told
He lay in weakness like a swooning flower
For six months' space, and thought from anguish passed
To feeble cold that seemed a dreamy death,
And afterwards rose up to pallid life,
But gained no vigour and no noontide strength.

' Then came a sort of vision,' thus he said
Unto the Priest, 'the sequel of my thought
And brooding, not a dream.
                              It was a cross
That rose between me and the morning heaven,
And held a Sufferer pale in quivering pain,
Yet holding back the writhing and the throes ;
And heaven seemed darkening, and the weary sun
Grew wan and faint as in bewilderment,

That could not gaze upon the Sufferer's pain,
Nor dared to gild the thorns which gemmed His brow.
But fascination, even while heaven grew dark,
And horror, kept the Features and the Form,
And cross, clear-marked before my sight ; so clear,
I seemed to read the expression on the Face,
And saw thereon a purpose shaped and kept
Through even the anguish of the taunt, that round
Seemed ringing mockery forth . . . and o'er me came
Thought like the utterance of a far-off voice,
Which told the meaning of the cross and dark . . .
I knew in caitiff's crown of thorns the King ;
And knew in guise of malefactor's death
The holiest thought and noblest wish of man.

'And from the dark came forth a hand that held,
Stretched out unto my grasp, a wreath which seemed
Like His of thorns ; and near the hand a voice
Like still suggestion of unspoken thought
That said, " If thou wouldst follow, bind thy brows
With this. So His triumphal pain shall fill
With fire of noble impulse all thy heart."

'I put my hand to grasp, and then drew back :
For as I reached I saw the marble Face
With quiverings crowded. In suppression even
Of these the fierceness of the pain stood forth.
A shudder shivered through me, and " Divine

It is," the thought within me said ; "divine,
But yet the clasp of suffering unto death,
Too great for mortal strength and mortal brow."

'The hand and wreath from vision slow withdrawn
Passed into darkness ; then the cross and Face
And glimmer that had lit the Face.   And dark
Sank on my heart that homeless in the dark
Was fluttering, as a child in straggling moans
Amid the wild at night its mother lost.
'Twas He, I thought, was meant to give release,
Not burden ; rest, not toil ; and joy, not thorns
For crown.   And with my thought the darkness grew
A deeper dark.   My thought sped on—it seemed—
The dark.   And somewhere in the night a voice
Spake, and it said, "The thorns are joy, the toil
Is rest, the burden is release.   But grant
That these they were not, wouldst thou dare to use
Divineness of such death for only self?"

'And then I felt the Face to heaven was raised,
And as with lightning cleft the bitter dark,
With voice ineffably forlorn, " Eli,
Eli, lama sabachthani," echoed through.

'And shame welled in me, boiling up to move
The encasing mud of self-regarding wish.

And then once more the hand with offered crown
Came forth, and voice, " Make offering of thyself
In love of men for service of that love,
And link thy deeds and fate thereby with His."

' My hand I stretched and took the circling pain
And therewith bound my brows.   But shaking limb
And fainting thought were sequels of the deed,
Till strength somewhat returning seemed to bring
Thought equal to its task to do and bear.

' But then again came suffering, heavy, long,
And weakness.   And the heaven was crowded o'er
With doubts which cloudlike kept its daylight back,
And oft return, and hide its peace from thought.'

The Priest, a quiet speaking in his tone,
Gave counsel.   ' Be but patient, and with face
Turned towards the light, seek stedfast for the light ;
The Heaven grows clear to those who wait the hour
Whose destiny is dawn.   The dark remains
To those who, leaving patient search, shut out
The light with curtained thought that night is round
And has an ending other than the dawn.'

XI.

THE ENGINEER'S TALE

ANOTHER day,—their friends beside them sat ;
And they were listening to the tale of climb
Recounted with the marvels of its hours.
—The wondrous silence of the starry night
And snowy sea that blushed at smile of dawn ;
And cliff with ruin lying at its foot,
The heaped memorials of its greater past,
Which stayed to tell how destiny such as theirs
Was watching for the rock's most inward strength
With agelong patience, changeless, moveless, calm.

And in the balmy eve when eve grew dim,
And o'er the mountain-snow its death-hue stole,
And heaven was hung with pall of purple-dark,
The Engineer at wish of all—but voice
Of Belford spoke the wish—began his tale.

'It was my lot to guide, awhile agone,
The joining of two shores which face to face

Stood fronting each the other o'er a sea
Which, here a narrow arm of three leagues' width,
Bore petulantly to its wider deep
All essay at approach by silting sand.
Two headlands stood, the guardians of the line
Of either strand, and where the racing tide
Beneath them rolled, it rolled across a ridge,
The lowly wreck of what was once a bond
Between the shores, by hunger of the waves
Devoured.   But underneath the liquid roll
It stretched, with here and there a jutting head
That, fathoms deep, had longer patient borne
Its battle with its ocean-enemy ;
On these were placed the towered foundation-piers
O'er whose high tops the iron road should run :
Caissons, that to their destined goal were towed
Afloat, for firm enrooting on the ridge.
These, poised above their resting place and sunk,
Were freighted at their base with prisoned air
That, heavy with compression, met the wave
As equal, holding back its liquid mass,
And barred its entrance to the chambered keep
Wherein men fixed the caisson's foot, that thus
Was formed to tower, root-fastened to the rock.

'Of these the midmost on its bed its mass
Had just reposed.   And on its top I stood
And watched the sun with yellow flood illume

The veil of cloud wherewith it hid in heaven
Its parting hour; and in the yellow burned
A darker tinge as amber mixed and red,
And all around the light-filled veil crept clouds,
Dull joyless clouds—nor even a languid smile
Lit up with rim of light their inky shade.
Then 'neath its canopy the night grew dark,
And all its hollow slowly filled with voice
Of rising wind, which drove the beating rain
In squalls before.   The next day laboured up
Sullen, resentful, brooding, heavy, dark;
And o'er the wondering waters crept no smile
But dull long roll of wave pursuing wave,
And in the later morn the rising wind
Howled itself into tempest, till the air
Became one roar, and sea one seethe of foam.

'And o'er the caisson broke the rush of storm,
And howled around with howl that swept away
The sound of voice, and beat the swinging crane,
And rocked it to and fro :
                        No chance to make secure
The shifting gear : when effort failed and risk
Was useless, underneath the topmost stage
We sheltered, bolting fast the heavy door.

' The caisson shivered to its very base
Where labouring hard the workmen strove to fix

Its foot. To them at intervals I went
Through door and air-lock down the newelled stair,
And with encouragement of cheering words
Sped on their toil. And ready hands and hearts
Toiled steadily and well the forenoon through.

' But in the early afternoon the shock
Of storm outstorming all its past with crash
Came on. The shaking caisson's wind-side rose,
And on the lee the foot crushed down the rock
Whereon it pressed. The crumpled floor in heaps
Rose up unto the base's half-way line ;
And sliding down the yielding rock the tower
Bent forwards from the wind and surging wave,
And from beneath the tilted foot the air
Boiled upwards, bursting through the bounding foam;
And in the gap it left the waters rushed
And swept asudden, deluging the floor,
And in a moment all was dark and whirl,
And then eventless silence.
                              I my voice,
To quell the fierce suggestion of my fear
Uplifted, seeking answer from the dark,
And voice and voice amid the darkness came
In answer. Bidding one to seek the stair,
And from the upper stage return with light,
I called the names by one and one of those
At toil within the chamber : answer came

From all. A moment's cold of sweat came o'er
My brow, and shiver through me ran. Relief
Was almost swoon. The light descending showed
Each face thinned pale. I bade them one and one
Ascend the stair to gain by respite strength
For later toil.
         No more there came that day
Such burst of fury, but the wild day sank
To sob of eve, and sob of eve to sleep
Of windless night. And only moan of wave
That could not cease its utterings of remorse
Around the caisson wailed.
         The basement then
Air-filled again to drive without the wave—
I searched the cause of sliding and discerned
Where weaker bedding of the rock and joint,
Unequal to the pressure of its foot,
When wind and wave made heavier still its thrust
And somewhat changed direction of its strain,
Had crumpled 'neath the pressure and let slide
The heavy bulk. The morrow's sea more calm
Gave chance to mark the caisson's rightful seat,
And move it, tilting gently, to its home.

'And through the day and through the morrow's night
I stayed to speed the toil and make secure,
And change to frequent the relays of men
Whose hastened labour in the prisoned air

Brought quick exhaustion on.   When all was safe
I sat upon the caisson's deck awhile
To rest rug-folded.   And with sudden hand
Sleep seized me, and it led me unto dream.

  ' Black space was round me, yet with studded isles
Marked o'er, some points, some orbs, and one there was
That grew and ever grew in widening blaze,
And seemed the sun in awful growth, but pale
Beyond its wont beheld through air of earth ;
So large it grew that o'er the vast expanse
It stretched as floor to half the sphere of space.

  ' And from the crystal chamber where I watched,
I seemed to see that floor's expanse of fire
Come nearer still and nearer, and a fear
Within me stiffened all my flesh and hair,
Till something stayed the approach, and fear, begun,
Died into wonder at the awful scene.

  ' Above me rose a whirling cloud of mist
That poured its downward rush of spangled hail
In columns like the spout of waters seen
At sea.   And looking where the columns fell
I saw below me seething lightnings massed
And matted thick unto an ocean face,
Whose waves for crests had tongues of whitest flame
Which writhed and quivered, shot from side to side,

And all around an endless roar arose
From out that deep : a roar of many sounds
And many notes and many mingling tones,
That seemed, some new, in new vibration waked,
Some older, some from centuries afar.
So strong, so soft, so near, so far the sounds,
They waked a harmony whose majestic voice
O'er-thundering many thunders deafened not
Nor stunned, but roused the ecstasy of awe.

'I gazed in fascination on that sea,
And as I gazed I saw a storm of flame
Tornado-like, except that by its side
Tornado were a crawl of pigmy breath,
Rise upwards, whirled unto the height afar,
And there aglow it hung awhile, then, dulled,
Became a mist that spangled in the light
Poured upwards on it from the ocean's face,
And glistening like a jewelled canopy
It spanned the height, then, whirled in eddies, grew
To cloud, whose massed array of glittering points
Heaped themselves unto larger, and rained down
In lustrous shower of gem and metal snow
And crystal, hued with hues of many tints.
And some in rapid rush of midmost fall
Glowed into drops that beat upon the sea,
And some still crystal smote its fiery waves,
And where they struck a steam of coloured flame

K

Arose and wandered upwards ; and all round
Mounted and ceased not from the heaving sea
Flames that if folded round this world could wrap
Its bulk to hiding.   Ever and anon
From spot and spot rushed fierce tornado up
And fell as whirl of elemental rain,
And heaven, aurora-filled, sent flashes forth
To track their path amidst its crystal mist,
Where chasms, but few, in the rent canopy
Revealed the distance of that upmost mist,
And awfullest dark of empty space beyond.

'And through that mist a wandering portent came,
And tore an awful path amidst the cloud ;
A globe in fiercest madness of career
Rushing athwart the height.   The cloud it tore
Fell to it hanging like a trailing robe,
And underneath its path awhile the storms
Stayed their incessant rush upon the sea,
And left abyss of an unwonted calm
Of fearfullest expectation in their stead.

'Then on the sea rose up the leap of waves,
That with their mountainous tide pursued a path
Straight underneath the portent's frantic course.
Heaped up in awful longing for the prey
They followed till upon the horizon's bound
They curtained out its sinking with their flames.

And following on the tide such huge abyss
Was opened in the lightning-sea, that earth
Hurled in with forty other mates, its peers,
Would sink therein, nor choke the mighty chasm ;
Into whose deep there streamed, in torrent stream,
Cascades of flame and crystal cloud and mist,
Borne in by whirl of wind whose mightier sweep
Sucked up the wild tornadoes round its verge,
And rolled, like foamflakes off the sea, in drift,
Huge continents, and hung them o'er the abyss,
And flung them to the chasm's further brink.

'Across the sea that moving chasm drove
And dragged its trail of dying sobs, each sob
Tornado of tornadoes.   And not yet
Had died the fury nor had time to die,
When from the opposite horizon's bound
That orb again arose, but nearer now
And fiercelier dashing through the cloud that writhed
Its mass, convulsed, to an enwreathing robe
For that new fascination.   And beneath
Still fiercelier clomb the mountainous sea and strove
To reach the orb and followed up its path,
And down behind, in distance like a heaven
For depth, abyss was opened.   Spasm of storm
Racked all around and all abyss and height,
And tore the very heart of mountainous waves,
And whirled their writhing mass to foam of flame.

'I saw the rushing world pass once again
The horizon-rim, and then once more come forth,—
Desire of flames up-stretched to meet its rise,
That lit the sky through which it rose with hues
And glories and with spiral glow of shape
So vivid, so surpassing in their gleam,
The light behind the glories, else intense,
Was wrought by their appearance shadow-grey,
And glows and hues of sunrise seem, in thought
Of that, to fade to lightless, hueless, dim.

'But as I looked the globe burst forth in flame
And made new thunderous music in the roar,
And hurried, slant in course, to meet the thirst
Which heaped the mountainous longings of that sea.
And, sequent, grew unutterable storm
That now was lightning-sea, now, whirl of foam
Fire-flaked, and now was torrent-flash, and now,
Cloud, and now, awfullest abyss : abyss
And sea and cloud and foam and torrent mixed
In one chaotic whirl of maddest roar.

'Then midst the fierce confusion wildest-thronged
I saw that orb with its out-flaming trail
Dash like the dipping seagull into waves
That welcomed it with burst which seemed to break
And shatter all the mighty sea, and flared
Through all the lacerated roof of cloud

That, torn to shreds, was scattered, driven far ;
And shook the shuddering vast of measureless space.

'And here I woke and saw the rain of fire
Shot by a falling meteor o'er the sea
That just before with thunder roar had burst.'

XII.

'UNTO THE HILLS'

THE morn which followed held the hour that struck
The signal for their homeward way begun.
Calm, clear, a morning pure with summer's sun
At summer's ending, and in golden light
Steeped underneath the cloudless blue. Alone,
Awhile along the road that wound and climbed
Above the steep of torrent's bank and floor
Of valley, Runimont to gaze his last
On height and stream and valley wandered slow.

But feeble sign that wore improvement's front
Gave hope of health to come. The hope of rest
For brain and strength for wearied thought, in vain
Was nursed within him. Weakness taunted still,
And taunted unto uttering of farewell
That spoke unto those mountain-heights reproach
As unto things which gave no aid, no love.

' I turned to you for voice whose potent spell
Could stir the numbness of my brain.　Ye gave
No answer, ye were silent.　Unto thought
Raising her languid head and grasping hand
Of hope, who with persistent tone averred
In you was restoration, and in you—
The long desire of childhood's years and youth's—
Was rest, ye gave but silence as response
To her that sought as though from human heart
Response.　And icy in your cold of day
Gleamed peak and snow with statue's moveless heart
And answered nought.　Adorned at dawn and eve
In cruel beauty, for yourselves alone
Ye donned the weaved bedizenments of joy
And answered naught, but let your silence bind
Pale thought the more to widowhood of grief
At her own blankness.　And in calm of night,
Whose unimpassioned stars gazed down on snows
And ice and lakes that stared their coldness back,
Ye answered naught !
　　　　　　The hour is come to go—
I go away, and ye are but a dream
Hung tapestry-like round memory's walls to show,
Not life, nor love, but only empty form.
I go without a smile from you of light
To wake in thought's wan eyes an answering smile,
I go away—and ye are but a dream.'

XIII

GRANTA

'SING it again . . . it may be as you say—
A morbid strain—a harmony of sighs—
It is to me a solace and a rest.
Shadows hang dull about my clouded brain.
Will ever sunlight clear return to thought?
Or is the darkness near when she must lie
Enchained upon the midnight soil, and speak
Only to utter sound, of meaning lost,
Unto the phantoms she creates and deems
Beings of life? and love pour fancied woes
And fancied joys to wake an echoing voice,
Where sound returns no echo? and the shade
Of reason, jabbering phantom, to and fro
Wander at scourge of feelings that have lost
Their power to find the object which they seek?'

There was no singer, and no song was sung,
But Runimont, awaking from a dream,

With which his fevered sleep had ended, felt
Vibrating still the chords he heard in dream.

Eight months had passed succeeding their return.
Flaxton and Wake still stayed and Runimont,
In Granta's home of learning.   Belford, Spring
Had seen remove to new abode of toil,
To give to medicine all his active power.

But Runimont by illness that cut down
With ease the strength so long impaired was chained
To long endurance of his prisoned months,
And now just raised as if on infant step,
And insecure and tottering like a child,
He shuddered in the torture of dismay,
Lest Thought should fade to shadowy feebleness,
And Reason, like a skeleton, only hold
The form disjointed of its links and power.

Yet slowly back both Thought and Reason rose,
Though not unto their former height of place,
Nor gave a promise yet of such return.
So seemed to him that life was path of pain
For him who had not strength to toil, nor hope
Except to suffer weakness to the end,
And dead hopes stared their dead stare in his face,
And anguish raised its bitter cry to God.

'Give what Thou hast for me, and I Thy gift
Will take though it should sear my heart, and pain
Be all the guerdon.   But I cannot see
Thy face to read if what Thou giv'st is love
Or anger.   Which, O Lord, uplifts Thy hand?
What holdest Thou in the shadow in Thy grasp?
The band that binds the martyr to his pain,
But not to pain of death, but pain of life?
To life's long cell of night, but not to joy
Of flaming car that takes him to Thyself?
Is that Thy gift?   Then let Thine hand impart
The martyr's thrill of grapple with his pain,
And let the light of victory in Thine eyes
Pour on my heart the rapture of a will
That in its rapture overstatures hope,
Lest anguish force my loosened grasp to fail,
And that be loosed which Thou didst give to hold.'

Through all had Wake's affection silently
Supplied the sufferer's need, whose lower purse
Had else been drained.   And many hours did he
In loving watch beside his prostrate friend,
And many hours did Flaxton sit.   And oft
When other duty gave the interval
They spent their time within his room to cheer
His days of slow recovery, till his strength
Sufficed unto departure's hour of pain.

Two days, and then departure from those scenes
Wherein affection roots too deep its roots ;
So near the end was come.   What years those years,
What past that past had been ! what brought ! what
    wrought !
And yet is absence exile of the heart !
Two days were yet ere Runimont's farewell ;
The Priest, in hope by solace to assuage
Somewhat the sorrow of the parting hours,
Had come.   With Runimont he wandered round
Amongst those courts whose age-robe like a garb
Of lichen hangs its beauty on their walls ;
They trode the ample court where Newton dwelt,
And passed the chapel-side whose inner space
Is thronged with memoried names of those who knelt
In worship there.   They passed the screens and strolled
Through Neville's cloistered court, and reached the lawns,
Then went beneath the trees whose tall arcade
Arched the long vista, till the tree-girt road,
Dyke-bordered, lay beneath their feet.   And there
They downwards gazed to see the pictured heaven,
And pictured light, which dark-hued waters hold.
Where topmost trees in early evening's light,
And downmost branches, dark in shade, respond
Inverted, to the lowmost branch above,
And topmost gilding of the sunlit tree ;
And sweetness and the calm of heaven below
Give answer to the light-calm heaven above,

O earth, can even thy dyke-slow waters, stained
With tincture of decay so picture light?
So glow with peace? so show the far-off heaven?

   They looked across to leafy walls which stand
Above the Cam, and foliage trailing down
To reach the stream and kiss its dusky face.
And over all, o'er foliaged wall and tree
And lawn-sloped banks, the buildings of the past
Rose in their varied outlines softly clear,
And bells that sang for evening chapel gave
A voice expressive of some distant peace,
Some distant hope, some joy afar but sure,
Some far-off victory, some far-off rest.

   And as they strolled along, 'These were my haunts,'
Said Runimont; 'these, since the shadows closed
Around the hour whose hope was living glow.
First here to me she dawned; her form of light
Long labouring through the massive bank of cloud
That wrapped her round. But gathering strength awhile,
She tore the swathing dullness, and looked forth
From her celestial home 'mid flame-red locks,
And seemed as bent to conquer, and lit up
The scene to life's horizon with her glow
Of bright-hued promise, then hemmed in again
Fell back into the dreary grey of day,
And left the landscape hueless, veiled, and dull.

The voices of that past are quivering still
And press upon the present.   Old thoughts speak
And old ideals voice themselves with word,
Old longings cry—but all as with the tone
Of a dead voice in phonograph stored up
And speaking of the past as in the past,
And memory seems as if in act to tear
The coverings from her coffined slumberers—
The past is past—why should it wake again?'

'Is life to you, my friend,' the Priest replied,
'Only the tomb of what no more can be?
Only a fugue repeating o'er and o'er
With changes sorrow-noted its own past?
And has the present only hope to spend
Its efforts in a wail o'er what is gone?
Let not your will in helplessness lie crushed
Beneath the swooning form of wounded hope—
Bid it be patient and arise, O friend,
Wait but awhile for strength, and bid it rise
That it receive aright what meaning lies
In all that bars the onward path, and tread
To victory.   Bid it arise and use,
Not fail beneath the trial.   Could the rock
That towers to catch the glow of morning sun,
And throw the gleam upon the dawn-dull pass,
Be dowered with strength to spurn the tingling cold
Of clutching ice, and macerating drip

Of dribbling stream, and the expanding heat
Of summer's forceful sun, without its past—
When titan forces pressed it in its bed
Of hope-lorn proneness mercilessly down,
And in the sweat of anguish held it crushed,
Until its inmost atoms, tortured, writhed
Into new combinations?   Thus, made strong
Beyond its compeers, adamantine-willed
It rose upheaved to face the myriad years
And scorn its frost foes and the dalliance
Of heat; while in its fellows casual stream
And shower found scarce-resisting easy prey,
And bore them into final waste.   This teach
Unto your heart, and bid its patience live,
And unto your hereafter let your past
Be not a dream inconsequent of deed,
But school of greater things.   Low lies the heart
Which lends itself unto the foot of cares
As pathway.   Feebly speaks the string of thought
Upon whose slackness strikes a nerveless hand.'

' I know,' said Runimont, ' I know the truth
Too well of all.   No words from other lips
But speak less clear than does the bitter speech
Of lips of slow experience whose face
Melts to no human feeling, and I know
That if the guerdon of but one success
Were the glad destiny of will and thought

Resolve would seek again her olden strength,
And thoughts now wrapped in powerless infancy,
To vex the mind their mother with their limbs
Of shrunken waste, would rise as brood of health.
But like the spell which on the limbs in dream
Drags back the hastener from his aim, a spell
Lies cumbering will and mind and thought.'
                                        ' Then wait,'
Replied the Priest, 'and, waiting, hope, till work
Becomes a thing which does not mirage-like
Go on before and keep itself unreached.'

' That have I done,' said Runimont, 'and do :
But wait like one who holds beleagured fort,
Not hoping for release, and knowing well
The end must be to sink o'ermatched in death ;
But holds to help his country's cause.   Like him
I bid my will endure and toil till death,
But think not of success beyond this meed :
Endurance to the end.'
                        ' Then thus endure.'
Quiet and low, yet full of all that fills
Counsel with strength, the Priest's voice said, ' Endure
To conquest.   That which tongues pronounce success
Is but a showy garment which at times
Result, for more display, throws round her form,
But greater than the glitter of its robes
The living form they wrap ; and spurning these

She oft seeks souls with whom along a path
Lowlier but nobler, dearer to her heart,
In garb severely simple she may walk
And unbedizened.   See you hold not deed
At valuing of repute that follows deed,
The blame or flattery which the changeful crowd
Bids or forbids; but judge it by the laws
That are eternal laws of right and truth.
So do; so patience keep; so wait the end.'

XIV

THE DYING SCULPTOR

AUTUMN let fall at touch of winter's cold
The wand she held, and bade the woods be clad
In garb of changeful hues.   And spring arose
In glad young strength and smiled, till winter's cold
Gave way beneath the beaming of her smile,
And she with laughing voice of windy stir,
That shook the leaves, pursued by summer passed,
And hid herself to wait another year.

A few brief days—they seemed to friendship brief—
The friends together spent.   The Engineer,
The Priest, and Runimont, and Wake, and next
The man of Science, Flaxton then, and last
For briefest, Belford, not alone he came,
And welcome much was given the bride he brought.
A hostel on the gentler slopes that front
The snowy heights at which they gaze from far
Was where they met.   Around, the leafy trees

L

Let through wide gaps the distant dream, and rich
In foliage wrapping all the hostel's walls,
The creeper waved its trailing arms and spake
In love-low whisper as the breeze went by.
At eve in gathered group they sat to talk,
And as they sat the Priest rehearsed the tale
Of one whose tale not long before had wrought
Itself its sad accomplishment. His voice
Beginning, other voices all grew still.

' Low in the hope-lorn twilight of that room—
Twilight it was within though day without—
Lay he I came to see, and lay alone ;
And I drew near and saw the dreary dream
Of eyes that in large gaze from out their caves,
Sunk in the whiteness of a face shrunk back
Upon its bony frame, took what they saw,
But, listless, for no information sought
Of what they took, but only, as I moved,
Followed my movements, as an infant's gaze
Half-sleeping, follows moving light. I reached
And took the hand stretched helpless at his side,
And added to excuse for entrance words
Whereby intrusion sought in service given
The answer of acceptance. Unto this
His weak lips gave their murmured thanks, but more,
His eyes ; though there I saw a sorrow rest
Whose shade the gleam of thanks could scarce illume ;

And few his words in answer to my words,
And to my questions little his replies
Gave answer, and itself the room told more ;
Traces too clear it showed of conflict waged
Against its fate of poverty and death
By genius which in victory wounded fell.
The clay stood there which finger-pressed was left
To stiffen into death of rigid shape,
When from the work his hand could grasp no more
He crept to lie where he had since lain low.
Of all but barest needs the room was bare,
And scarce of even these it held the signs,
And help or comfort for the sick was none ;
But, from their stand, unto the hollow face
Of him who made them, turned his visible thoughts
In moulded clay and looked their changeless look,
And held their moveless limbs, and spoke their love,
And told their sorrow, and their calm of ire,
In moveless dignity.   And in his face
Sickness I read, but more than sickness read ;
Famine was there, awaiting, as I saw,
The moment's near approach when she could light
Her fire of fever.   Drug nor nurse at hand
To help, and on his lips, in low response
To all my questions, words whose meaning mocked
The weakness of his voice, "no need of help
For ailment light and soon to pass away."

'I stayed but little time. With feigned excuse
As of appointment made whose hour had come,
Entreating leave thereafter to return
I left the room, and with the granted leave
Gained chance to bring the help which soon must come
For even short respite—else would come too late.

'Of fitting food and help secure, again
I sought the room, and through persuasion slow
Attained success, by little to impart
And little, drops of food. And on my steps
One I had sought—physician he and friend—
Followed, who came, he said, to seek me here
On matters bent whose bidding could not wait
Uncertain interval of my return,
But in the sequel of excuses turned
As with new thought to know what illness here
Had asked my help, with other questioning,
Which sympathy new awakened seemed to prompt.

'I turned unto the sculptor's face, as there
Seeking the answer he, not I, should give,
And then my friend, with question more direct
And tone of interest growing in his voice,
Drew slowly from the silence and the words
Of him who stiffly held in silence all—
Save what his feelings felt uncouth to keep—
The knowledge that he sought, and gained at last

Reluctant leave to listen to the voice
Wherewith his beating heart its message sent
Through breast and limb; and note the whispered sign
Which travelled through the corridors of breath,
And test the burning of the flame of life.

'Thus, careful of the wound of noble pride,
We carried all the bastions of his will,
And brought unto his weakness aid of drug
And tendance; and more face of comfort gave
To the bare room, and curtained out its dearth.
But more than this we had no power to give—
The life to every effort wrought gave back
An answer of delay, too short delay,
And hope not even evasive gave reply,
'A moon, a moon or so, and then the end.'

'And somewhat oft I sought the room with him,
Who pressed the pleasure of his tendered skill
Upon the patient's still unwilling heart,
Which persevering tendance made to glow
At last with welcome. Somewhat oft alone
I went and sat beside the dying man,
To give the respite of an interval
To the assiduous nurse, and cheer with words
Of solace, if a solace were, the heart
Of him from whom all comfort seemed so far.

'And thus some days went by, and then his tongue,
Released a little from its famine-chain
And moving to the thrill of friendship, grown
Now strong, revealed the story of his life.

'An only child, whose parents long before,
By sickness hurried through exhaustion's gate
To death, had gazed their parting gaze of grief
On him they left an orphan, friendless, lone :
His way along the thorns of life had lain
Away from kin, and nearer seemed than kin
The friends and even the strangers that he knew :
For only distant kin at distance his,
His father and his mother sole remains
To those who bore them of their birthling group ;
The rest had closed in death their infant sleep—

'He told me how when first the sense of form
Like revelation of a glory came,
It filled his heart with eagerness that spoke
As if the voice were destiny's, and awaked
New longings that impelled him on and on.
He told me how when music on his ears
Was poured, it woke arrays of forms that filled
The chambers of his thoughts and seemed divine ;
And how from toil to toil his spurred resolve,
And goal to goal, in ceaseless quest advanced,
And power had seemed to come with stroke of tool ;

But more reward than barest sustenance
Came not to aid his labour-driven thought.

' But yet at times, for very joy of toil
He laboured on, whene'er the shaper Thought
Unveiled her quick creations to his hands ;
And even, at times, despair of giving shape
To that which floated all divinely clear
Before his thought, impelled his will the more
To break the barriered fence which daunted hope.

' His way—the long, long length by penury dogged—
He toiled to Italy Rome-wards.   There at Rome
What seemed awhile the auguries of success
Floated about him, voiced with thronging hopes,
But changed their wheeling course and spake despair.

' And here upon his lips not words that moved,
But quivering came, and I in silence sat
Until his trembling voice resumed its tale.

' "A friend," he said, "came one day in and led—
Asking to see the shapes my studio held—
A group to me unknown, but friends of his.
And of the group was one whose form of grace
On the sweet verge of ripening womanhood,
And voice and stately gesture, drove my thoughts
Upon themselves confused.   A strange delight

And stranger fear encaged them, and my words
With them, that beat in helplessness like wings
By fluttering birds bent frayed through prisoning bars
For exit : stammering thought gave stammering word.

'" To me, before that hour, had form appeared,
When form was beauty, like a thing divine
Whereon I gazed with awe that kept my thoughts
As kneeling worshippers, but there came then
A newer thrill, a newer awe, a joy
That stretched its seraph hand to thrill with pain.
From kneeling unto prostrate sank my thoughts,
And yearnings, whispered in my heart before,
Broke into cries.   And perfect form that stood
Afar before to take the worship given,
Sublime and cold, made new approach in her,
And looked direct upon the thrills it woke,
And, looking, roused the thrills to ravishment ;
A sacred joy in feeling of unworth
To share the honour so bestowed welled up,
And while it humbled seemed exalting more.

'"She came once more, and yet once more again,
And I, as in the spell of some sweet dream,
Forgetful of all other thought or form,
Found *her* in all imagination worked,
Found *her* in every hint emotion gave.
New shapelings flitted frequent into view,

That were each one some sweet suggested joy,
Fashioned upon the living clay of thought
By gestures and by movements which were hers.

    ' " 'Twas like the end of weary pilgrimage
In a sweet land of sunny blissful peace,
Whose clouds sailed love-winged through a love-clear
    heaven,
And boundary hills afar through lucent air
Showed their calm dream of cities height-enthroned
Above the lowly sleep of sweet champaign,
And one long rim afar of distant hope
Spake low the sweet suggestion of the sea
Love-lit, love-billowed, there, unseen but sure,
Lengthening the unseen distance with far joy.
A land whose birds poured melody through the day,
Like that which from their nests they chirp at eve,
Love's sleep song. Evening's splendour sank to rest
At serenading of the still sweet night,
That filled its sleep with dreamy thoughts of peace,
And melted into blissful morn that lit
The verdure with the jewelled lace of dew,
And filled the heaven with treasured light, and rose
With distant song which echoed forth the strains
Sung sweet in dream. And sunny day brought lull
In all its sleeping light and restful shade ;
A lull was on my thoughts that lost themselves
Adream, and lost, except as shades which moved

And voices that without a meaning spake,
All knowledge of the world around of men.

'" But, like the distant mumble of the snow,
Broken and speeding to its fateful fall,
The news fell on my heart that she was gone,
And then the increasing thunder and its crash
Beat on my brain, and dashed my buried thoughts
Down depth and depth in wild enveloped fall,
And in the sequent silence all was dark.

'" Gone ! all my power and all my life was gone,
A self that seemed a sepulchre and held
Some dead self's corse was what was left behind ;
The very air of day clung close and choked
With pain of breath—room, room I sought and breath,
And beat with gasp the walls that stifled space.

'"Gone ! And my heart that in its moveless dream
Of joyous awe had been to such a thought
As any end oblivious, and no word
Had dared, nor even a sign that spake of love,
Was filled with stings that turned upon themselves
And stung and stung in madness of regret.

'" But worse than even the stinging of regret,
A lash of bitterer thought enforced a calm,
Cold reasoning calm, a calm like that which comes

When down the ice-browed precipice of alp
The cragsman, slipping, sums with lightning speed
Event and chance before him, and his glance
Surveys in those few moments all of hope
Or all the death that is his rushing fate.

' "Speak unto her of love? How should I speak—
The starling to the eagle speak of love?
To what reception would the high-born maid
Admit the words? A cold surprise of stare
From her were like the stroke of bitter death,
Nay, aught which unto chill of distance changed
The stately kindness of her present seemed
That it would fill with torture all the hours
And all the future years. An easier fate
It were, upon my prostrate neck to feel
The pressure of her foot that trode my gaze
And lips into the dust that foot had graced,
If this could mean compassion, than to speak
And bring the death of all that could be hope.

' " Yet rose at times regret in fevered rush
And held a maddened struggle with despair ;
Was there so much in blood and high descent
That scorn were certain end of ventured love?
Was high-born heart so distant from access,
So far aloof from what could give it joy?
Her eyes had hung upon my work and filled

With rapture as they gazed, and smile had lit
Her lips, as turning to my face she showed
Reception of the thought upon the clay
Impressed, or sculptured on the chiselled stone.
And when she gazed upon them I, thrilled through,
Had seen the look of light which grew like that
Of one in hope and happy love adream
Upon her mate when he is far away.

  ' "And could she love the shapeling thought and turn
Cold scorn upon its shaper ? Speaking thus,
Doubt brought up anguish gasping in my throat,
And misery unto weakening palsied thought,
And hateful were the weary days and nights
And blank.   And hateful was the voice of men
And harsh and grating, who, not shadows now,
But loud, intrusive, hustling, seemed to press
And trample on the wound that laid me low.

  ' " Then sickness smote me that my feeble thought
Wrought as in stupor, dreaming that the shapes
Of its dim fancy equalled those its toil
Of earlier years created – dull, dead dolls,
Shapeless, not even grotesque she saw them, waked
Once more at end of months, but waked to *see*,
Too feeble to *create*—and horror came
And dread.   Had power for ever left my brain ?
Had destiny for my end a nameless grave,

Unto which goal through wilderness she led
My useless steps? 'Twere better far at once
To lay me in the desert than drag on.

'"But strength crept back, and when it came I rose
To meet my fate. It were not just to her
To venture even to bind her life to bear
The loss of all that she must lose for me,
Though such Elysium as her love would bring
Should be the sequel of my love confessed.
Be silent then, let silent love pour out
Its unavowed expression and its strength
In work the better done for love of her,
And dream, for satisfying of that love,
That she would let her eyes upon my work
Rest with that loving light mine eyes had seen
When she—and I was near—on it had gazed,
And with some kindly thought would dwell on him
Who worked the shapes which gave her soul delight.

'"What memory held still clear of that fair face
I wrought in stone as stay to soothe my heart,
And often round the neck have held mine arms
And spoken to those cold lips, and pressed thereon
The reverent kiss which was not meant for stone
But dared not hope on more than stone to rest;
At times unto my yearning fancy seemed
The face as melting to return of love."

'He pointed to the bust.　The face, I saw,
Was placed to meet his gaze as there he lay;
It was a face whose noble lineaments,
Imperious in their beauty else, revealed
The writing of a tenderness which spoke
As almost with a living voice, and thought
Imprinted there seemed more of heart than mind,
Though imprint clear of mind was also there.

'"But it was all in vain," he said, "in vain,
It has been all in vain, and hopeless love
And bitter anguish of regret have broken
My days, and almost has my madness reached
At times such strength that I was fain to drag
My anguish in confession to her feet
And ask for what I felt could be but death.

'"I loved, and never had that which I loved—
Had I possessed and lost, my grief, meseems,
Were easier borne—if even a single hour
Of that which I must pine for till I die,
Her love, had smiled upon me, then were fate
Less dark, less crushing; but to love and feel
A stony silence all of love's return
Is fire that in its lightless flame torments—
The fire of something worse than a despair."

'He said not more.　Exhaustion's weary drops

Stood thick upon his pallid face and brow,
And on the skin-loose framework of his hands.
I wiped away the drops and gave him food,
And held the trembling hand which clung to mine.
No word at first I spake—what word had I
For solace unto such a fateful grief?

'But when with food and rest the trembling ceased,
I ventured question who she was, and where,
If he yet knew. And in the answer learnt
'T was one of whom I knew but knew her not,
But once in days when she was child had seen.

'And as I left the room that day a thought
Came to me like a floating leaf which clings
Wind-pressed upon a garment's woollen front—
It clung and held and would not loose its hold.

'I doubted if my steps might go the way
O'er which that thought held out its pointing hand,
But ever when the doubt came forth to hide
The signal, upwards rose the thought and held
Its finger sternly forwards in command
To that within which answers duty's call.

'It bade me seek the maid on whom such thoughts
Of love were poured. I started on the quest
And gained the meeting sought. Such face and form

I wondered not should wake the love, yet wake
The awe which kept love silent in its spell.

'In answer to my earnest wish she gave
An audience to the tale of want and woe,
Which first I told without its secret note
Of love, and gained expression of distress
At want and sickness crowning genius thus
With poison-wreath of death.   Then point by point
I made my way, and led her memory back
To know the sufferings as of one to her
Not utter stranger ; then at last unrolled,
But cautiously, the story of the love
And worship rooted in the dying heart.

'Astonishment and silence, at the first
Were answer.   I with eyes upon the ground
Sat in suspense.   When I at length looked up
I saw the imperial beauty of that face
O'erhued with paleness, and unnoticed tears
Stole down their silent way, and unrevealed
By word, emotions stirred within their shrine
Of maiden heart   I sought not what, nor felt
A right to seek --so one I sought came forth—
Pity—which came and grandly rose and filled
Her heart and with its impulse checked the voice
Of pride, and in true human garb looked forth
And sought out comfort for the heart which soon
The voice of comfort would address in vain.

'She bade me as from her supply in full
Whatever comfort lacked, whatever need
Required, and made appointment of an hour
Wherein to meet me at the sculptor's side,
And somewhat shyly, yet with voice whose tone
Showed greatness reigning queen, she gave to me
To take what more than all, she felt, would help —
Pledge of her coming soon—her pictured face,
Wherein his dying thoughts a present joy
Would find.
      And this her gift I took, and took
The promise, and with cautious words and slow
Unto his listening told my deed and tale.

'"Twas like the waking of the dead to life
That heard not at the first the voice which called;
But after faintly heard—then more distinct,
And hearing woke. So grew his face to smile
Of joy from its wan shadow of despair.
His feelings, keen with reverent love, took in
The meaning of the visit and the gift,
As if by intuition, finely true—
Not even in fondest dream his hope had held
Such prize of joy, nor did his grateful thought
Seek more return to glad his dying heart
Than such sweet sympathy from her he loved.

'The hour was come—and living face and look,

M

Not marble's fixed response of eye, returned
His gaze—the marble at his wish was gift
To her, accepted as from him when death
Should end his need for marble's memoried form.

    ' His eyes looked up to hers, and spoke in light ;
And all the thin white face with grateful joy
And reverence shone.   It seemed as if I saw
An angel smiling from beyond the bourne
Of life with love that made approach from far.
And she her face bent down to his to gaze
In such sweet passionless love as like reply
From answering angel beamed.   When I, as oft,
See o'er again that scene 't is like a glimpse
Of some new world, where love is glorified,
Shadowy in form, but of transcendant might.

    ' What glory gilt those afternoons with joy,
Wherein her visits came, and lit the morns
With zodiac-light of sweet expectancy,
And gave his nights their silent requiem—peace.

    ' The moon was scarcely past.   His pallid sleep
Was plainly floating him to brink of death.
We sat in silence as she stayed to see
His open eyes if, opened once again,
They made return of gaze.   I saw her stoop
And lightly with her lips his forehead press.

The kiss, before her face was raised, awoke
The sleeper, and he knew what just had passed—
He smiled as one whose eyes surprised beheld
The earliest glimpse of heaven.   Death caught the smile
Before it passed, and shaped the grateful glow
And silent calm of that pale wearied face
Into the semblance of an angel's sleep.'

XV.

EVOLUTION

THE eve before the group broke up they turned
To him of Science, to beguile the hour
Of dusk with somewhat from his learning's store,
And thus in turn he led their listening thoughts.

'I wandered through the world of living things,
Seeking to understand what is, what was;
And wishful in the varying multitude
To trace the laws which rule the growth of form.
Long time it seemed I trode with useless steps,
But at the end I heard a voice which said,
"Not outward semblance but homologous part
Must be your field of search: For structure, like,
Shows kin, and, unlike, hints remoter kind;
And function is interpretation's guide
To show what is homology of parts."

'I looked, and lo the world of life was grouped
By that new thought unto its kinds and kin:

What else had seemed a random scattering,
Unmeaning, planless, then arrayed itself
To groups and kindreds each with settled post.

'Again a voice, which said like quiet thought,
" Likeness in growth's successive stages shows
The same descent." The thought lit up the path,
Obscure before. The youngest shapes of Time
And skeletons of the past, the embedded dead
Of ancient rocks, took up their several posts.
The deep gave forth its forms to join the array
From out the mystery of its thwarted light,
Even to the lowliest shape of living slime:
Forms limited, not shaped, that gave not yet
A prophecy of symmetric shape—nor more
Than segmentation leading slowly on
To more complexity of larger whole;
And all stood forth in rightful rank and place.

' But then came lower, and so low, I heard
But part and not the whole of what it spake—
A distant voice. " Life and unlife are linked,
And to interpretation of the whole,
Unlife and life in one, these four lead forth—
Inertia, function, kin, environment ;
And dower of fittest tendency o'ercomes."

' But dim and dimmer grew my thoughts, I seemed

Steered outwards in a shadowy bark afar
To unknown coasts, whose filmy headlands rose
From out a hazy ocean ; then still on,
To pointless movement on a fog-bound sea,
O'er which at last a thought rose up and loomed,
But rose not o'er the fog in steady pause,
It gave through gaps a glimpse and then was lost,
And I was borne to vaguer, dimmer dream.

    'A solitude around, and utter blank,
An infinite of nothingness, nor near
Nor far a goal, nor near nor far a point,
By which to trace direction or approach
Or growing stretch of distance ; nor was Place,
To give suggestion of " beyond."   For " near "
Was not nor " far," nor aught by which itself
Movement could know as movement, nor the lapse
Of " then " to " now " reveal itself, and nought
To show the embryo " now " as passing phase
In the evolving of " to be " . . . a pause,
A sleep or death of movement, force, and place,
Expanse, dimension — nay, of matter's self,
And even of that whose interaction builds
The mystic building " matter."   Not one thrill
Feeblest of feeble passed the awful void,
Not one last trace of gurgle, as a sun
Disintegrate and dark, was lost, dissolved
Into the undimensioned nothingness,

No whisper of a dying system's breath
Rippled its last, its faintest, through the vast.
The pause was like the pause in blank of swoon
Between two conscious moments, dreamless, deep,
A silence which mysterious faintness told,
And that alone, as other than a death.

'A blank, unsphered to space by studding stars,
Blank dark, unthrilled by vibratings to feel
Duration, and unintervalled to time
By aught of oscillation, or of phase
Of what might seem to go or to return.

' Then something, how I knew not, seemed to steep
The blank, nor whether slow it came or quick
I knew, but what was blank became therewith
Chaos of influences that teemed, obscure,
But gave to thought the vague, the infant hint
Of blank whose awful stillness intervalled
Cosmos and Cosmos. And as infant stare
Looks on the moving things around, nor knows
Distance at first from sequence, so knew thought
Not then, if that most stirless silence lay
Between a Cosmos that had had a past,
And one whose whole existence was to come,
Or two existing and isochronal,
Or two in part coeval ; and the blank,
Ocean of nothingness between their shores.

'And then there came to thought the feeble dawn
Of power which aided her to grope her way
Towards the concepts Time and Space, and these
Gave the arena over which dim forms—
New concepts—passed like titan shadows thrown :
A death of something past whereof no sign
Disturbed the dark and blank ; a birth to be
That gave as yet no sign of coming throe;
Concepts whose shadows firm and firmer grew
Until they reached to definiteness of form.

' For those awakening influences that stirred,
Seemed in mysterious movement, as results
Awaking from a sepulchre of sleep,
Renewed to newer phase of infant life ;
Infant, not inchoate—renewed, not new ;
But yet they stirred them, as delirium's thoughts
Half shaped, that crowd each other and rush on
In jumble of unsettled path.   There seemed
No hitherwards of moving sway that woke,
Nor thitherwards.   Confused unmeaning force,
Scattered and mixed and jostling, with no bent,
Nor even prophetic tendency, to point
To settled course or rhythm or gathering shape.

' Then came, as when from vague delirium's dream
Thoughts trace their way to reason, that which gave

Impress of aim which slowly shaped itself
To certain path. And in the vast afar
Grew glimmering haze, that in slow change became
A cloudy light; and as the light grew more,
The chaos filled about with thrills that moved
In complex movement, rhythmic as in thrall
Of subjugating law with destined aim;
And slowly changed the light to shape defined
Of spiral glow, that later knit its streams
Into spheroidal fire oblate in whirl.

'And ever in the blank afar some streak,
Some haze, some cloudy film of light appeared,
New, one succeeding other, till there glowed
Ten thousand shapes diverse of nebulous cloud :—
The blank became the studded sphere of space.

'But measureless in age, for awful length,
Seemed the slow moulding of the dawning haze
To spheroid fire, unmeasured as the dark
From which that haze had crept. But now I knew
The wreck of a past cosmos in what filled
The dark of blankness. In the blank I knew
The death of what had filled a measureless past,
A death which to a newer universe
Was birth, and gave it in that silent throe,
As heritage from its mother's dying pulse,
The embryo bent of destiny which shaped

Its progress through unmeasured length of age
Unto its death in the eternal-far.

'And, as I watched, the spheroid fire, grown large,
Brought forth its mighty progeny, evolved
Through ring and swarm and globe to planet suns—
The embryo brood of millioned years—that rolled
Their titan forms around their parent globe
Which shrank and shrank in giving birth, but blazed
The brighter for the pang of lessening self.

'One of that brood I watched, to see its growth :
Begun as hazy ring of floating light,
Which, when its infancy of ring was past,
And youth of spiral gyrating, that closed
In spheroid orb of slow maturity,
Wrapped round itself even such a film of ring
As it itself in infancy had been ;
And gave the 'minished story of its birth
In that new child which grew to sphere and rushed
In wilful course around, and lost the glow—
Its dower at birth—and colder grew and shrank,
And, shrinking, rolled in wider path, and changed,
Till, parted far, a cold and blistered ball
Spinning with slowing gait, with wandering worn,
Unable to return, it turned its face,
In changeless lassitude and late regret,
Always unto the parent it had left

In wayward wandering ; like a child whose eyes
In dying turn towards its mother's face,
And so remained in the still calm of death.
And while the child thus changed from wreath of flame
To rigid cold, the parent world, sphered more,
And gathered more about its lessening self,
Flung out flame-stretchings of embraces huge
Towards its retreating child, the awful thrills
Of wild emotions in continual tide
Rending her breast with mighty billowing sighs,
In vain attempt to press her parting kiss
Upon the child whose wilful slow retreat
Fulfilled itself in far remorse and death.

   ' But when the child out-distanced all the reach
And gurgling of her woe, and grew more cold
And let emotion show no visible sign
Of living thrill, but only held before
The moveless mask of dead emotions past ;
Earth's parent breast grew less disturbed and less,
Slow-yielding to her long despair.   And age
From her withdrew her glowing light of youth
Until the ash-scarred remnants of her fire
Of fierce primeval passion lit no more
The space around her, save when here and there
A fiery sob of wailing passionateness
Broke through the sullen stillness of her breast
With earthquake throb.

But age by age there came,
Even from the burstings of those fiery throbs,
New drops of anguish which at first she drove
In steamcloud from her scornful breast that brooked
No taint of weakness, and flung off afar
The signs of tears and oozing sweat of pain
With titan hiss; but after, when the strength
Of fiery eagerness grew, aging, less
They fell upon her bosom --even thus
To meet with fierce rejection.   But at last
Grown weary she permitted their approach
In wreath of moving mist, and then in wave.

‘ But when, as oft, she felt her weakness sting,
Or when her parent sun unwonted thrills
Sent, that were fierce reminders of her past
Of fiery power, she raised the lash of winds
And drove them whirling forth that would not leave
But ever clung.
                          So æons crept away.
The passion of remembrance of old strength,
And passionate longing for her wandering child,
Grew calm, and earth with less reluctant breast
Submitted to the mellowing influences
Of the vast sea of waters, which remained
After the wild emotions of her past,
As signs and oozings of her agony ;
Whose soothing slow caress, and soft embrace,

Endured at length, brought thrills unknown before,
To haste the aging stupor of her grief,
That so her scars felt their hard surface veiled
With film of lowliest plant, which o'er them spread
As if with healing hand of peace.   Her seas
Filled all their longing depths with lowly hope.—
Earth woke to feel the primal touch of life.

'New rapture, destiny new; whose eager rush
As of revulsion in the heart, broke forth
With an impassioned fulness, to produce
Its multitudinous new variety
Of mode and form and structure, till at last
The rock-thronged mountainous throbbings of her storms
Of passion, grown in act of throb to stone,
Began unto the stimulus to yield,
And spreading plains and nestling vales and slopes
Were robed in lofty plant and diapered stem
And feathery foliage thick with quivering hopes
Responsive to the wooing wind.
                              Thus passed
Through long-continued change the pictured world,
As through a series of dissolving dreams
That led still onwards unto newer change :
Free-moving life, and moving things to haunt
The forest green, and things of wing to flit
From plant to plant that carpeted the ground ;
And shape and tinge and tender pencilling

And hue in sweet gradated shade began
On their tipped verdure—means of that strange link
Which binds the plant unto its birthling plant.

'And things of moving life began to feel
The stir of new sensations which came forth
As feeling, vision, hearing, after growth
Crawling through generations. Then arose
In later forms of life the mystic sense
Which thrills to passion. And the green recess
Of forest and the stretching plain were thronged
With other sound than sweeping wind—with voice
That had a meaning in its changing tones.
And slowly memory rose, and—acolyte
To memory—reason, and the complex mind ;
Till, in the monarch of the throng of life,
Passion and feeling grew to nobler selves
And blossomed into love, and mind assumed
Intelligence and consciousness. And birthed
From these came moral sense and sense of shame
That unto their possessors contact new
Gave with the universe of things, and gave
Resource which wrought them power of search and power
Of use ; conception that subdues and guides.

'Thus earth unrolled her scroll of destiny,
And, all the ages long, her parted child,
The moving moon, beyond her parent aged,

Evolution.

In calm and stiffened cold, but lovelier
In her death-cold, poured down her calm of smile
Upon her parent earth—a borrowed smile,
Which when the storms of life to moveless peace
Of death have sunk, shines on, not from, the face.
And still the sundered earth in yearning gropes,
But gently, for her unforgotten child ;
For with such lower tide emotions roll
Across her breast, as seem but stir in sleep.

'Here let me end—at least this evening end—
The story of the universe is long,
And all too complex is its tale of life.'

XVI.

MAN MORE THAN REASON

THE chorussed thanks of all were heard, and then
  The Priest began :
                    'With much delight my thoughts
Have at your leading tracked the mighty strides
Of one development, amid the throngs
Of many millioned orbs that ceaseless roll
As denizens of the measureless vast of space :
One—type perchance of destiny of all,
But type, perchance, as life in lowly forms
Is type of life of man.   A destiny seems,
Like viewless tide that yet is stern in flow,
To sweep the bark of all creation on.
Whence comes—the thought within puts question forth—
That unreturning tide's determined flow ?
Whence came, I ask myself, the destined bent
Which gave the embryo-cosmos law of growth ?
And whence, as much, the bent that guides to-day
The future of the embryo flower or germ
Of animal life ?   I ask myself who know

Man More than Reason.

That such poor contact as the mind can have
With all that is, gives but one surface-touch,
Nor more than one interpretation's voice
To that which may have meaning manifold,
Or range of meaning wider than the ken
Of mind, as wider than the ken of sight
Reaches the spectrum-range of solar ray.

' In that life-tale repeated ever new—
The germ's reiteration of the past
Of its far-reaching ancestry, concise
And brief and outlined, which its being writes
As prologue to the drama of its life—
I seem to see one instance of that sway
Which reigns through all the universe of things :—
Permanence in direction and advance ;
Result, the sequel of continuous steps,
And not a sudden entity, upsprung
Without a link to bind it to the past—
The path by which the end attained is reached,
No easier has annulling, than long ranks
Of centuries on the roll of Time—
                   Through all
Is permanence in direction and advance,
And deviation from the right-lined course
Of repetition ever of a self,—
The deviation complex influences
Force, that themselves vicissitude of path

Have felt in thrall of some directrix-rein,
Or some new influence to themselves akin ;
Whose ending, through acceleration slow
Of ages, is a course, remote in pace
And conformation, from its primal start.

'Advance, continuance, permanence, result—
Not linkless spasms nor self-engendered throbs,
As if of matter that were self-upsprung,
Matter, the limited, that could not rise
Into spontaneous assonance, self-create :
These surely speak of impulse by some Power
Distinct from Nature unto Nature given :
These surely speak Creation, and themselves
Are parts of that Creation which they speak.

' And though such thought bewilder, it, I deem,
Leads not to such inconsequence complete
Of supposition as awaits the thought
Which feigns a Nature of itself the cause
And of its law of being.   Though I know
"Twere reasonless to deem for Nature need
Unto her being and her destiny
That they be comprehensible to man :
What cannot be, man only in one sort
Can judge, nor is he measure of the whole.
No finite cruse exhausts Infinitude.

'These impulses of Nature signs I deem,
And impress of a Power which shapes the mode
Of every birthling Universe His Thought
And Will engender ; Him, I deem, from these
His thoughts, in personal separateness distinct,
These His and He not them.
                              And " He," I say,
And " personal separateness," and, saying, feel
As if a lisping child would strive in words
To utter some inceptive thought that comes
And flutters near and floats away, too huge
For grasp, in cloudy maze.   For saying " He "
Of that Eternal Will, I use the word
And know too well, that Personality
Of Infinite Presence and Eternal Power
Is limned in feeblest outline by such terms
As paint with easy stroke all powers of man.

'But would express, by terms like these, belief
That He whose roll of thought is Universe
Succeeding Universe, is such that these
His thoughts, in Him have part like man's in man,
Nor span the might of His Infinitude
More than do man's successive ponderings span
The power and life of him whose passing states
Of brain they mark ; but that they bear to length
Of His eternity such length as bear

Man's separate thoughts unto man's sum of life,
Who lives beyond their evanescent term.

'And I by saying " He" would say that power
Belongs that Infinite Being, which controls
The long array of Universes birthed
One from the other, with such sway as man
By will exerts to fashion or destroy
Over the shapelings of his brain—save this :
Man does no more than group—that Power creates.

'This palimpsest, this cosmos bears, I hold,
Throughout the impress of the Hand that writes.

'And also saying " Personal " and " He,"
Thus argue : to that Infinite Power belongs
Existence which from all that is besides
Sunders that Power, as consciousness and life
Do man from things that have not life as dower.'

' I have no yea to say, and yet no nay,'
Replied the man of Science, ' to your thought.
If there be cause—then, what that cause may be,
Or whether cause is part of matter's self
I say not, cannot say; for natural things
Have naught that can of more revealment show
Than of themselves, and of themselves they give
Part only; there the knowable has end.

'You spoke of thought, you seem to speak of life
As, in some fashion, property of Him
Who is, in your regard, the Cause of all ;
But thought is comrade of a form of life,
And all we know of life is as it were
The flame of act of combination, lit
By ceaseless change and kept by change aglow ;
Between such ceaseless, necessary change
And changelessness like that you give to Him
Yet call it life : between such passing state
Of brain in living things as thoughts and that
Which you conceive in Him—yet call it thought,
Is nought and can be nought of parallel.'

' Is nought of parallel full well, I know,'
The Priest replied, ' but neither is there aught
In all the shapelings of the tongue of man
To serve for that delineation's truth
Which these, though in the dimmest way, suggest.
They are analogy only, faint and dull :
But if the words give such poor aid alone
As shows a partial truth, and are as far
From truth, as from coincidence is far
The circle, small of orb, that meets the rim
Of one whose ampler sweep leaves separate soon
The smaller ; still the words, defective, weak,
Are what we have, the likest and the best,
And with what words we have as fittest tools

It is our lot to shape the thought of Cause
Who plans and rules the destiny of all.'

'If that you need attempt to shape such thought,'—
Returned the man of Science, 'but so wide
A chasm is placed, without a bridge to cross,
Between the shore which mind of man can know
And that far shore of mystery profound
Whereto such thoughts attempt to take their flight ;
That what you reach must be a guess too dim,
Too shadowy, to give shape to any dream
Or adumbration of that cause unknown.'

'"If that you need !" but there are hearts that need.'
The Priest with lighted glance of feeling spoke.
'They throng the generations of the past,
They throng the present, and what sign appears
To show their future fixed diminishing ?
Lives unto which the need is hope, a hope
Without whose spring their thoughts and acts sink down
In joyless, dull despair.   That need, meseems,
Is in no less degree interpreter
To tell the first essential and the cause
Of all that is, than Reason is of law
In natural things.   A need that cries aloud
For love and truth and goodness in its God,
And sickens unto death before the thought
Of one who like a Phantom, all unknown

In attributes and power, commands its way
Of comfortless silence to a mystery
Of unknown bourne.   Instinctive is the need :
As much instinctive and as much a need
As is the mother's love, which never lack
Makes less a normal thing, though there perchance
Be lack in any mother of that love—
Which is no work of Reason, though, with gaze
Thereon directed, Reason may tell the cause
Why it exists, nor does she more produce
What feelings else within the heart of man
Instinctive work ; they came and entered first
The portal, she with after-step came in.
And he who thought to give, as if complete,
Description of the life of man, and trace
The source of act, yet thrust out these from view
That, more than Reason, prompt the deeds of men,
Would fail, and show no more than part alone.
And in their narrow field, these, part of man
And part, as much as Reason herself is part,
Afford a hand to gain some grasp of truth,
If truth be that which *is ;* so there but be
Interpretation of their meaning given
In its right harmony with Reason's voice,
Or such as clashes not with Reason's note.
Man is not Reason only—man is more.'

A FAREWELL

UPON the morrow's morn, on Belford's knee,
Just as the voices ceased that spake adieu,
At starting of the post-chaise, Runimont
A packet placed and what it held was this:

'Farewell! 'Tis we to whom the parting pang
Brings dark and cold—thou hast what lifts the light
Above the waves of sorrow, nay, will hang
Stars hope-lit o'er its gurgling sea of night.

'The voice and eyes that give thee sweetest rest
Thou with thee hast; be long thy lot to hear
That voice to thee of music tunefullest
Speak to thy listening heart its love thrill clear.

'Thy lot be long to have those eyes to thine
Their sweetness of devout affection bear,
To have that love its buds of peace to twine
In every flowerless wreath of thorny care.'

THE LEGEND OF THE VANISHED STAR

THEIR halting place was close beside a lake,
Whose waters in the morning light shone pale
And glimmered like the waking of a smile;
And there the long day's sultry length they stayed,
For the green waters stream-fed from the ice
Of glacier gave the thirst of heated air
Sips of their cold.   And in the afternoon
Came low the thunder-wraith, and crept the lake
With trailing cloud, and poured its floods profuse,
Swamping the meadow verdure by the shore,
And streaming on the lake's pure green a flood
Of turbid wave that, mocking the disdain
Wherewith the clear-hued deep received it, stained
Its face far out.   So on to end of day
The cloudy torrent whirled itself to swell
The turbid throngers of the lake.   Awhile
At sunset ceasing its impetuous grief,
The storm grew still and held its flowing skirts,
As gazing on the gold-thrilled rose of eve,

And listening to new chord or thought of hope,
Which tinged the dulness of its gloom with joy :
But when the horizon-hidden sun no more
Could lift the glory of its parting smile
Face unto face, but only threw o'er heaven
Remembrance like the smile that lights the dead ;
Then waking from its rapturous reverie
It poured anew into the echoing dark
Its streaming torrent of repining thoughts.

And thus the hours grew long, forbidding aught
Except delay.   Round Runimont the group
Was turned to listen, as he with quiet voice
Gave the fulfilment of desires that long
His friends had shown by utterance of lip
And iteration of the uttered wish ;
His lay the legend of the vanished star.

' I sate within an abbey's ruined wall,
Its chapel wall, whose ivy-robe of leaf
Clothed it for fresco : moss and grass and fern
And bramble decked its floor and upward crept
About the bases of the columns, hid
By lichens in their tender lowly garb,
To cloak the ravage of their moulded lines.
Wounds, windows once, gaped silent in the walls,
Their tale of grace and beauty lost for aye ;
Except that one where eastward once it crossed

The light with branching beauty still retained
A fragment of its tracery unto which
The climbing ivy reached and sought to give
Its clasp of sympathy—a welcome clasp.
The wearied fragment seemed to feel the love
Which brought the leaf in kindliness so close.
Above its responds, still the chancel arch
Kept its high watch and showed arcaded walls
Facing, on either hand, the trailing grace
Of rose and honeysuckle that, like wings
Which held the ark in shadow, filled the spot
Where the high altar stood.   I sought to dream
The abbey's past, to see the rites which erst
Were celebrated, and to hear the chant
Of voices sounding to the timbered roof :
To see the hooded throng in slow array
Pass up the echoing nave—but sought in vain.
My wilful thoughts strayed off from rite to cell,
From cell to toil of labouring scribe, from this
Unto the pages of an olden book
Hand-written on its vellum leaves with ink
Of black, and here and there with red adorned.
The toil of one who in such home had lived,
Whose faded ink and olden-lettered words
Deciphered told me tales of olden years ;
And one therein there was whose broken thread
Was full with fascination to the thoughts
Of those who wandered down its faded lines :

For here and there a line in clearness left
Stood like a fragment of a picture, else
All veiled to sight, and stirred solicitude
To see the whole, but tantalized nor gave
The chance, nor could all effort reach to more
Than this decipherment of what it held;
It was a legend of a vanished star.
But pondering on the fragmentary tale
I lost myself in dreaming—this my dream.

' Fairest and best it gemmed the crown of dawn,
Hung there to thrill her hallowed dream of light
When first the dawn from out the pristine dark,
Rose like a bashful maiden closely veiled
To light with joy the earth and new-made sea
And heaven, and crept in shyness up as one
Who feared the gaze of that to which she gave
The light to see. And best and fairest gemmed
The crown of dawn that star. But when the dawn
In later years rose pale above the sin
And violence of earth, and earth was filled
With curse of wrong, the star had lost its light
And gemmed no more the dawn till He was come,
Whose childhood was the world's new dawn of life.
Then new in that new dawn its herald light
It gave; and through His childhood shone and lit
With lustrous joy the heavens, while still His voice,
Ringing with love and longing like a prayer,

And teaching clear the faith He held in pain,
Was heard of men. And earth seemed roused once more
To sweet remembrance of her Eden prime;
And all the yearnings of the age-long past,
Long crushed in blood and lust and rapine rose,
And all the weary prayers and all the pain
Which all those centuries through for love and peace
And purity had cried, but trodden down
Had sunk to ashen coldness, seemed anew
Awaking into fire in human hearts—
Seemed waking—but they seemed to wake in vain.

'And earth lay in her shadow of despair,
But with the moon to give the silent light
Of hopeless smile to light her wrinkled face.
The stars shone pale behind her pallid fire,
And heaven wheeled round their glittering multitude
Like steady tide of uncomplaining grief.

' Night, . . . with the moon to give the silent sign
Of hopeless smile . . . *that* night the traitor's lips
Had pressed the sop which sacred fingers gave,
And shameless from the room of Paschal Feast
Had gone to work his treacherous thought to deed.

' No thought in those the traitor left within
Unto what purpose gone he took his way
Thereout into the moonlight's shuddering gleam;

Save that beneath the guise of friendly smile
The Master knew the traitor's heart, and knew
The horror and the insult and the pain
That for Himself the Iscariot-steps would bring,
But turned His face towards that pain of death
As to a mighty joy, and unto those
Who near Him saw His features glory-lit,
As with the triumph of a coming throne,
He spake what left His lips like seraph strain
Of ecstasy. Then leading forwards trode
With feet of conquest on the opened way
That led direct unto His agony.

'How wan, how weary is His face, how pale
The scattered glimmer of His anguished eyes,
His languid form, held rigid unto toil
Of prayer in pain, is quivering through with throes—
And yet He sinks it not to earth to rest.

'I see upon the pallor of His brow
An oozing stain. . . . It drips from off Thy face
O Christ, but Thy clasped hands held close in prayer
Regard it not, nor cease their clutching clasp . . .
He bows His head. It meets the dew-cold ground. . . .

'Long thus He knelt, prayer-bowed with face to earth :
And from the westward heaven where evening light
Had died there came a star, that nearer drew
In constant flight and bright and brighter seemed,

Held in the grasp of one whose robe streamed out
Like a clear web of floating light of moon,
And form was angel's and the star, him close,
Was in his grasp a chalice glowing clear.
And bending low on reverent knees, with face
Awe-veiled by love, that angel-form the cup,
Flashing like lighted crystal purest white,
Offered unto the kneeling Son of man.

'And of the cup He drank, but as He ceased
Some drops of that red flow which left His brow
Fell in the cup, whose light that sacred touch
Of anguish sudden changed from crystal white
To crimson tender-pale, whose glorious hue
Glowed sweeter than the sweetest light of gem.

'Straight to that scene the traitor's footsteps came ;
But as he came the angel-form arose
In heavenward flight, and holding in his hands
The glowing chalice. Crimson from the heaven
Its parting light was flashed, and as the kiss
Of treachery touched the lips of sacred woe
The light was lost, eclipsed in sudden dark,
And thenceforth from the heaven was gone the star
Whose morning joy flashed o'er that sacred birth.

'And men looked longing oft to heaven to see
Once more its rays, and looked in vain, and left

The hope of its appearing once again
Unto the generations unfulfilled.
Thus the long hope was handed down the years.

' But at the end of centuries lived a monk
Ere mid-life worn to age by toil that sought
No boon for self, but in the use of self
To work relief for woe and aid distress,
And in effacing of all wish but this
Sought the fulfilment of impassioned aim ;
The fevered felt the soothing of his touch,
The leper knew his care, the tongue of age
In famine and in suffering uttered words
Of blessing, and the dark of dungeon foul
Had hid his form, but let into the light
The broken wretch whose place he took therein.

' His worn heart, beating with that one desire,
Reached in its long endurance of the strain
Unto more fevered passion, as his frame
More weakly grew, and self-devotion, stung
By its own spurs, began like frightened steed
To champ upon the bit of self-restraint.

' It was a morn of early summer's glow;
Upon a hill, and just beneath its brow,
He sat.   The toil of tendance in the night
And rush of thoughts, which, like a stormy wind

Fluttered the quiet dignity of will,
Had left him chafing unto wild unrest.
O'erhead the fir trees' groined embranchments hung,
And their dead needles strewed the summer soil.
And where the steep forbiddal of a rock
Barriered the trees, the light of morning crept
And lit with smile the moss-draped stems. The rock
Was near his seat, and its high outline stood
Tinted in hue of dawn. And soon the sun
Behind a fronting ridge, fire-pinnacled
With pines that robed them in the jewelled light,
Arose, dissolved the pines awhile in glow,
And underneath their foliage, midst the stems
Where long the stems had ceased to hold their arms
In hopeless withered stretch, shot forth a beam
That reached beside the sitter, lighting up
The rock, and tinging all the creeping moss,
Whose dewy coronal seemed to bud with fire.

'He, half in dream, as drowsiness of morn
Began to steal upon his restless thoughts,
When on his sight the sense of coming glow
Smote gently, saw, it seemed to him, a Shape
That o'er the morn's horizon purple-rimmed
Stood flaming, and the chalice crimson-pale
Was in his hand, and lit the sky and trees
And pinnacles and moss and silent rock.
And in the waking murmur of the trees

o

He heard a voice that came as from afar,
A voice like music whispered lowly-clear.

'" In vain, in vain, in vain, the earth once more
Is searched to find a willing heart to build
A temple and an altar where to place
The holy chalice.   All in vain once more
Are night and wandering through the sleep and dreams
Of men.   For morn and waking-will hold back
Intents that slumber till the night again
And dream renew the vision and the wish.
In vain, in vain, the earth is searched in vain !"

'"But wherefore?"' seemed a voice from far away,
From even the furthest heaven, to speak and ask.

'" He who shall build will build as unto doom,
And building he will build himself his grave."
Thus spake the answer, and the voice was still.
And then the second voice that spoke afar,
" But earth has yet its hearts that dare to greet
Anguish and death for Him who welcomed these
As meed of the deliverance of man —
Shall not the earth be searched yet once again ? "

'And as the words fell on the ear of him
Who sat adream, half waking from his dream
He spake unto the words he heard in dream,

"Behold the willing heart which greets the task,"
And knelt, and as he knelt he thought a voice
Replied, that said, "The task is thine." And sound
Of far-off chants seemed sung amid the glow,
Where died the cloud in glory of the morn
Dissolved.   He with the covering of his hands
Concealed his face, and his sealed eyes beheld
His thoughts and only these, and reverie left
When round him was the sunlight and the day
Sending its full morn's glitter through the trees.

' Was it then his, that task of worthy doom
Which pointed to the toil as certain grave,
But presaged not what suffering formed that grave?
His weary hopes leapt forth with joy to meet
The mystery and reward of such a fate,
'T was chariot-fire that seemed with glory's meed
Consuming whom it carried up to God.

' Three hours he knelt, and three hours thence arose ;
The building pictured stood before his thoughts,
A new impetuous wish strode high and held
His heart, and flung all other wishes back
Unto that trodden soil, the pathwayed past.

' The market throng filled, in the midmost morn,
The city's square, and thitherwards his way
He took.   Well known to all the throng the man,

Well known his voice, but not the tone that rang
As he before their upturned faces told
The vision, and the voices, and the task ;
And, ending, thus he poured his torrent words.

'"The task is mine.   It is not mine alone,
Nor could my hands, though they were worthy, raise
Alone a worthy temple, and my life
Were lengthened out to fill a hundred years
With ceaseless toil.   A boon I ask of you,
The boon of aid.   The honour and the share
In building is for all : for one alone
The death.   If consequence to all were death
I would not ask, would simply tell the call
For those whose will to such a victory led
To enter on the labour.   Life is meant
For willing hearts to mount to noble death,
But only to the willing is reserved
The seraph-thrill that fires to upward tread
Of will on that triumphal path.   The feet
Of others tread the road to idle death :
But think you idle death is worthy more
Than idle life ? that creeping feebly down
Unwilling to the dark is worthy end
To aught except unworthy path of life ?
'The mighty, not the mean, should lay thee low.
Do battle with the gods '—did not this stir
The war joy in our fathers' heathen hearts ?

Shall we be less than they when Christ has lit
With supreme glory such a crown of death?
Is His voice weaker, bidding us to fall
Or conquer, than the call of heathen heart
That bade him fall before some stronger foe?
To meet and conquer, or to meet and die—
Some mighty duty; this, not ease, is life.

'"But well I know that God in His high love
Gives suffering as that duty unto some;
And well I know that not to all is given
Such altar-burning of prophetic fire
Within the heart as strengthens for the task.

'"I ask for aid, and aid that all can give.
And say not that you wish not to speed on
The hour of death for me. I see that look
Upon your faces, and the lips of some
Are fixed and close, as ready to deny;
And some I see who, with their open lips,
Are ready with that answer to my words.
I am not that I was, ye know it well,
Ye that have known me stand beside your sick,
Ye know that patience answers not to will,
And will has lost its olden spur to push
The lagging gait of strength, and anger roused
Breaks in me oft the tables of the law,
When I behold the earth's idolatry

Making you sing your own destruction song,
And dance the dance to tune of ruin's pipe.
I am not that I was . . . and less the years
Show patient usefulness my future lot.
Better to work at something worthy death,
And die, than live among you with regret
Gnawing my heart that cannot help you more.
A boon it is I ask you.   If perchance
Succour in any wise from me has come
To any, let him do me this return
To help me to this mission of my death.

' " If there be he to whom in hours of pain
These hands have offered comfort, and his strength
Came back ; if there be he whose anguish-load
Of heart grew less at word of mine ; if he
For whom a festered limb or lame was wrapped
In bandage which sufficed to soothe or ease
What baffled healing, and his use of limb
Suffices for his need ; if there be he
To whom in famine's hour of low despair
Through me was given the cheer which roused to life ;
If there be those on whom in pangs of cold
My hands have wrapped a shelter, let them help !
The strength which knows itself a match for toil
Let it give offering of toil ; who lacks
Strength but hath will, let it suffice to give
His offered gift, and who hath treasured stone

Or wherewithal adornment may be wrought,
Let him bestow.
   And think not that I ask
As only for the boon for which just now
I pleaded. Unto me it is enough
To build and die the death of him who builds,
But unto you the worthy task is this —
That to the sacred memory of pain
Bleeding its tears of sweat in eager love
To give relief to pain and misery,
The hands of those to whom that pain of love
Has given release or peace should shape their thanks."

'He ceased.   The upturned faces rapture-pale
In dense peripheral lines their fervent gaze
Turned to his central vehemence.   At first
A silence like the waters of a sea
In moveless sleep lay o'er them, then arose
A murmur as the stir of gentle wind
Ruffling the silence ; then spoke voice and voice,
Lifting themselves above the murmurous sounds,
And toil and gifts in ready promise given
Their echo of united shout that came
Sent through the square and up the lofty walls
And tracery of the high cathedral spire ;
Which seemed therein to start anew and rise
In mellow music to the listening heaven.

'Zeal winged their readiness. The autumn sun
Lit the foundations laid with busy toil,
Where voice and vision took the sitter's thoughts.
The early summer morn on risen plinth
And moulded base for shaft-enthroned arcade
Poured its sweet light through mullioned apertures.
And autumn once again its sunset light
Streamed through the embranchments of the window
    heads,
Upon the shafts and capitals that bore
The voussoirs, centring-shouldered, moulded-deep.
Then spring, retreating at the summer's step,
Beheld the arch which leapt to roofless wall
From coronetted buttress-pinnacle.
And moon of harvest poured its dream of light
And slumber-depth of shadow on its floor,
Through rafters ranked and fixed in firm array,
And autumn glowed in sunset thoughts when late
She yielded to the winter's cold command
On roofed fulfilment of the pile that closed
Around the unfulfilled high hope, whereon
The years to be should throne the lofty wish
Of mighty tower and spire. One summer more—
On capital and corbel hung the shapes
And shadows of the beauty-chiselled leaves,
O'er which the softened lines and hollowed dark
And foliage band rose graceful that enhanced
The upward longings of the pointed arch.

'And he from out whose thoughts that vision sprang,
And rose from dream to hand-accomplished deed,
With tool which sped as driven by rush of thoughts
Pouring their torrent of created forms
So rapid that the execution lagged,
Wreathed round the choir its coronal and hung
From moulded groins their clustered leaves, and screened
The altar apse with lace of stone.
                                   Lame men
And maimed and weak, whose limbs no other help
Could render, worked with emulous will to give
Edge to his tools, or cleared away the dust
And heaps of stony fragments chisel-chipped,
Or brought him food and drink, or sat to gaze.

'And when from leafy shadow unto face
And lineaments of human form and mien
His labour passed, the rapt devotion there
Tool-wrought seemed almost to their listening ears
To utter prayer ; and to their wondering eyes
It was as if a present miracle.

'At last the altar's white of marble stood
Arcaded, and for shadow of arcade
Inlaid with alabaster yellow-woven
In undulating lines, and serpentine
Blood-red and lazuli and malachite ;
And studded round its rim with amethyst

And opal brought by pilgrims from afar.
Incessant had become his eager toil,
Day giving thought its shape, and night to thought
Giving her sleepless fever.   Even dream,
Filling the scattered hours of sleep, kept full
The torrent course of vision and design.
And paler grew his face, and seemed his flesh
To melt away around its bony frame ;
Impetuous fever driving on the toil.

'Thus came the day when chant of olden psalm
Sang out the consecration of the pile ;
When voice of prayer and chorus rolling up
Came mellowed back from soaring arch and roof,
As if on high repeated, softer sung
By voices more melodious than the crowd
That pealed their jubilant hymnody below.

'The rite was o'er, the last amen rang out
And died in melody to silent peace,
And through the echoing nave the parting steps
Of worshippers had passed.   The autumn sun
Flamed in the cloud-clear sky, and poured its rays
Through the rose windows of the west, and lit
With dreams of light the screen-defended choir,
And dreamy shadows floated through its space
From arch and corbel, canopy and pier.
But all the choir with tone and radiance filled

As if with thoughts of beings unbeheld
That were by new receptacle to eyes
Of men made visible.
    Knee-bowed in prayer,
And all alone, was he whose toil around
Arose. Exhaustion following on the track
Of effort's fever-fire.
    " Dimittis nunc
In pace servum tuum Domine,"
His lips had said, but in his heart the wail,
" Usque quo ?" rose.
    At once the western door
Burst open, and a shrieking herd rushed in,—
Women with eyes that from their sockets sprang,
And children in the middle years of youth,
And unarmed men. And following on the shrieks
The lifted swords that merciless cut down
The flying forms and strewed them on the nave,
And stained the level floor with flowing blood ;
Mauraders from the marches, unto whom
That festal day was new advantage, seized
Their chance, and sacked the city, and hewed down
The home-returning worshippers, and few
Pursued had reached that sanctuary's gate.

'Startled from prayer he saw the murderous rush,
And hasted forth with high forbiddal's voice
And stern appeal. He was too late ; the work

Of blood was done, and the marauding chief
Received his words with coldness, and to one
Whose sword was high to strike,—with blade outstretched
Warding the blow, he gave command to hold
".A weakling and a monk   let him go free,"
And, turning on his heel, he led the gang
Out from the open portal.

               Stunned, the monk
Stood in the light that therethrough spread around
And lit his stiffened form   that sacred floor
Strewn with dead faces whose pale silence spake
To him, their friend, of hours of solaced care !
Remembrances of help administered
Unto their living weakness—*he* debarred
From sharing in their fate, and kept to doom
Of ignominious life !   The grief smote full
His desolate soul.   Choirwards he turned his steps
That tottered underneath his load of woe,
And on the altar step a bitter wail
Rose from the lips that lay humiliate,
And to its coldness spake the agony
Of one who seemed forsaken by his God.

'A crystal chalice on the altar stood ;
And through a westward window of one aisle
The sunlight came and smote the oaken screen,
And one clear ray glowing through ruby pane
And through the screen's arcaded tracery fell

Full on the chalice, tinting it with gleam
That sparkled like a star of pallid rose,
And shadow tracery-cast dimmed all around.

'Just then the broken-hearted monk, his eyes
Lifting in agonized appeal to heaven,
Caught the red glow. A feeble gasp of joy
Broke on the sudden silence of his wail;
The limpid weakness of his weary eye
Lit up with smile, and spread its light of bliss
O'er all his pallid face, which with that smile
Stiffened in sweet placidity of death.'

XIX.

SOBS OF PRIDE

THE sweet September sun of one more year
    Lit their new journeyings through the mountain
    scenes.
And gilt the hoary summits, standing wrapt
In age-long stillness high above the pass,
Receiving ever new the messaged beams
Sent ceaseless by the unwearied sun, and these
Interpreting to their own poesy
Of silent evening glow, or morning fire,
Or glory of the noon, but dark in sense
At times when cloudy doubtful meaning spread
Its passing shadow o'er their brows, and dim
At times when more mysterious message came.

Along the pass to meet the Priest who last
Arrived the three strolled slow, and with the three
The man of Science. Wake, with face that bore
The look which comes when suffering gnaws the heart,
But borne in silence as within a grave

Is kept; and never word of grief he spake.
And Flaxton with the rightful pencillings
Of one year aged.   In Runimont the fire
Of life in marshlight flame once more rose up
With promises unmeant.   And somewhat thin
The locks of him of Science, but his step
Was firm, and eye was ready as of old.

From the high-seated hostel at the hour
When expectation sought the Priest's approach
They strolled to meet and greet their friend again;
Nor long before the hoof-resounding road
Gave sign of nearing chaise in dust upraised,
Nor long before his welcome countenance
Gladdened their faces unto welcoming smile
And waked the joyful greetings of their lips,
Nor long before the grasp of loving hand
Laid hold on hand, and from the chaise the Priest
Descending wandered slowly with them back.

They left the road a little while to sit
Rock-seated looking o'er the pass below;
Bushes around on which the Alpine rose
Mingled its stern simplicity of leaf
With just one lingering blossom here and there
Left from the sweet-hued throngs with which it clad
In earlier summer all the clustering rocks.
The dream of distance, Autumn's tender gift

Of young love's zeal, upon the landscape lay
In first and gentlest beauty, sign that speaks
Of near decay; but in its primal touch
Not yet suspected as decay, it tones
The harsh asperity of rock which stands
In indignation black to speak its wrath
Unto the soft and patchy snow that gave
Its virgin white to stain of summer storm,
And grovels as disfigured streaks beneath.
The air, fir-fragrant, from below sent up
Its evening incense balmy-fresh, and seemed
To win the Priest from his worn looks to thoughts
Of rest, but not secure and stirless rest.
As when the cindered crust that covers o'er
The lava-flow stirs sudden and reveals
The glowing anguish crawling on beneath,
And rustles shivering as it stirs—so showed
His face at intervals through outer calm
The signs of agitation and a fire
Within that glowed.   They noted, but not yet
Had asked revealment.
                              But unasked it came
In slow, sad words.   'Delay's excuse,' he said,
'I sent, but told you not what caused delay.
Indeed there was not time to speak the cause:
Brief summons when was yet an hour or so
Till I should start and join you, bidding haste
Unto a sick bed side; and interval

Of hours of journey lay between my home
And reaching that sick bed.   Unto your hearts
It is a grief I bring—but yet a grief
Whose cloud is rimmed with melting touch of light;
'T was Belford's call, and Belford calls no more.'

    A quiver ran along the old man's lips
As he then ceased.   The opened eyes of all
Looked on his face with stare of wonderment,
And Flaxton's indrawn breath prepared to meet
The enemy grief, as if there were assault
To come in detail of the history;
Wake's face showed sudden pallor, and the name
Like rapid spasm, ' Belford?' left his lips;
And Runimont with eyes in sudden mist
Of tears and choking throat, at utterance
Stumbled ; and sound came forth that was not word.
' How so?' the calmer voice of age's grief
In him of Science asked to know the tale.

    ' There was,' replied the Priest, ' where Belford dwelt,
One who in jealousy of Belford's skill
And rivalry unfair by stealth essayed—
An undeserving rare in medicine's realm—
To check the rise of his prosperity,
And prejudice was thereby led, for weight
Had been to this man's words aforetime given.

    ' But when in somewhat sudden sickness seized

He died, and left his debt-encumbered all
And children to his widow's feeble health,—
Improvident display had swallowed up
What else had been securing to his wife
Of barrier unto poverty's distress—
And sympathy, magnanimous of soul,
And pity wrought in Belford's heart and hers,
Whose wish was one with his, his wife's, desire
To offer for one child a home, and share
In such degree the widow's load, and make
New parentage unto their slanderer's child.

'But in few weeks the child grew sick, for death
Weaved the fell web whose leathery spume chokes up
The gasping throat, nor even Belford's skill
Availed.   His late arrival from the task
Of working almost to exhaustion's term
To root a sufferer's tumour from its hold,
Gave all too little chance to work success
In that which, when he left his home, had shown
No sign of being, nor was yet his wife
Released from out her room ; her birthling's days
Had scarcely mounted unto three weeks' space.

'What sadness and what grief can rend these hearts.
Honour and duty chained him to his toil
To save the child, when on his weariness
Unequal to the task the task was laid ;

And prudence and the safety of his own
Forbade the risk of even a loving kiss,
Or heart-exalting clasp from her, at once
So near, so far. But soon the hand of death
In merciless severity laid grip
On Belford's self, and weaved that rapid spume
In haste so fierce no help availed to save.

'A gasp of love that strove to be a word
His last, and one last look of peace that held
Its light above his anguish he bestowed
On her whose love, when voices told his death
As certain, flung command of absence down,
And staggered to his room, and saw him die.

' I led her back before relapse could lay
Its faintness or its swoon upon her limbs,
And the third day which followed saw the end
Of what my present service could effect
For her and him. Over the noble dead
That for his enemy's child gave up his life
I read the words of sorrow, peace, and hope,
The hope whose music-shiver curdling stirs
Emotions which can pale his lips who reads,
" I am the resurrection and the life." '

A silence minute-lived pursued the sob
With which the Priest had ended. Tearful eyes

Bent down but looked not at the Alpine rose ;
When sudden Runimont upleaping pale,
Paler than even a moment back, when sobs
Came thick ; and waving round his head his hat
'Well done,' sobbed out, 'well done, brave heart,' and
    cried,
In voice as of triumphant pain, 'Hurrah !'

And when the moment's stern astonishment
Gave place to understanding of his thought,
Upstarted all the group, and joined the cry
And voices as the tears rolled down their cheeks,
Strove through their sobs to lift their proud 'Hurrah !'

Stillness . . . and sobs . . . and stillness . . . and from far
Across the pass, from out the thickening cloud
Which, unbeheld while they were listening wrapped
In grief, had closed upon the mountain tops,
Came pealing back a chorussed loud response,—
The thunder shout of triumph raised by storm
Above its raining tears of grief to God.

XX

'RING OUT O BELLS'

'LOVED of the great, that with uncertain love
Gave answer to their longings, and too oft
Didst turn with jealous fury on thy best,
Who even in indignation could not lose
The love which lashed their anger unto more.
Loved of the great and mother; in thy shrines
What ashes lie, what memories crowd thy walls;
Firenze, O Firenze, beautiful
Even as a dream of painter's joy, but swept
Through thine uncertain heart by cold like that
Which from thine Appennines, when spring's warm sun
Makes hot thy sheltered nooks, sweeps merciless
Through all thy open and defenceless shade;
Such as thy clime, enchanting yet unkind
Wast thou unto thy sons, whose hearts were bound
In fascination of thy love, which now
Cheered them to victory of skill or thought,
And now cut down the effort fever-struck
By bitter cold. Firenze, storied still,
Though with the wrecks of thy past majesty,

Around the stranger as around thine own
Thy fascination throws its bond of chains.'

So Flaxton, brooding as he trode the side
Of Arno, that divides in twain the home
Of pictured thought and treading all alone,
And dreaming o'er the strangeness of the past,
And looking down Lung Arno's stately street.

And there in front approaching was what came,
As if a dream from out a past wherein
He seemed a part.   Two forms to something lost
Linked, and two faces seeming to recal
A shadow from days gone.
                         Some tide long time
Unstirred, some tide of thought and feeling mixed
Stirred inly, knowing not what way to move,
Yet agitated, as in act to take
Fixed bent of movement momently when given.

And then by memory's confusion roused,
Thought strove to find the impulse lost ; to turn
Its agitation to a flowing tide
Which knew its bent.   Motion at last and light
That made more clear the gravitating tide !

A grave among the mountains, and a grief
Pictured by memory gazing on the grave.

Thus came revealed from out the mist and dark
Of years their meeting in the pictured past,
And mutual recognition.   Greeting strove
To hold its stiffness, but perforce unbent
By memory, when from dreaminess aroused
She lit the past with sudden blaze of light,
And waked the olden grief to strength and life,
The stiffness changed to friendly thought, subdued,
But greater for its quiet of restraint.

And in the days that followed, unto more
That friendship grew.   On search together bent
Of Art's triumphal hoards of skill in church
And gallery and palace, they the days
Together passed, together went to view
The home wherein the infant Danté smiled,
And home of him whose thought had strength to shape
The early concept of a central sun,
And planet thrall to sun, and whose keen eyes
Through mean of glass and crowded thrill of light
Beheld the first far spectacle of worlds
In vortex-roll around their sovereign orb.

And Flaxton found a face that, when the hours
Brought end to such companionship, and day
Was melting into night, was ever close
And ever glimmered in the view of thought ;
The night with vision of that face was lit,

The day was lit to view that face alone,
And all too far the hour of meeting held
Its distance from the parting, and too short
The hour which parted marked the space that lay
Between the hour of meeting and itself.

And Painting, when that face was near him, gave
In whisper from the soul of her to whom
That face belonged what it before kept sealed,
The meaning of the oracle it speaks.
And sculptured forms their majesty revealed,
And light poured in, and life beat full where stood,
Before, the dulness of enigma's gloom,
Or moveless thought in stiff immortal death—
Shadow unmeaning and unliving stone
Took meaning and a life at touch of love.

So passed the days, and Flaxton seemed afar
Even from the few weeks' gap which intervalled
The last sad meeting with the Priest that told
Of Belford's death.   Their plans upon the sea
Of destiny adrift this year were driven,
For duty diverse in command had called
His friends, who listening to the voice went forth.
And Flaxton, left to wander, strayed alone
To find what wrought a newer loneliness.

So passed the days, and all but one had gone ;
The last, the sweetest, swifter than the rest

'Ring Out O Bells.'

In flight was come,—too swift and, like the light,
A crowd of agitations speeding fast ;
And hope and fear chequered the morning hours ;
And with the lingering of perplexity
Cold grew the hidden sun of clouded joy.

Not, as throughout the days that just were gone,
The joy of her expected presence changed
To fairer all the landscape of his thoughts.
But o'er it passed the shiver of a wind
Which swept his heart at times with bitter cold.

He looked, and then he looked not at her face :
Turned full his eyes, then in confusion bent
Upon the ground that spoke with no response,
But listening to the voice which swept with thrill
His feelings now of joy and now of pain,
He heard, and yet he heard as in a dream,
And sometimes meaning seemed to wander far
As if resentful of his brooding thought.

At last they came from out a church alone,
Together—and alone.   Her sister's steps
Had lingered where she stood to sate her gaze
Upon a fair Madonna's pictured face
That just before had chained both them and her.

' What sweetness was in that Madonna's face,'
The maid to Flaxton spoke when through the door

The twain had passed and stood to wait the third,
'The form alone would tempt the eye to keep
Long gaze thereon, but something more than form
Arrests and speaks. Love, which upon the lips
Just dawns in smile, seems in the eyes to speak
With pensive joy, but furrows on the brow
That hint at sadness seem in act to rise.
And how that kneeling girl her wordless prayer
Unto the face poured out in fervent gaze;
I wonder not that dwelling on a face
So pure, so sweet, so sad, so eloquent
Of love and pity, she should thus adore.'

'You wonder not?' said Flaxton. Rising up
Resolve within his heart gave spur to thought.
'I deemed the faith you hold had placed a bar
Before that wonder, and had named the act
Idolatry and sin.'
                    And she at once,
'I hold not with the act. I do but say
I wonder not that one from childhood taught
The worship of the mother of her God
Should see in such a face what there she seeks,
Should find response to instincts scarcely shaped
As yet to thoughts.'
                    And Flaxton, with a smile
That glowed as if behind the cloudy veil
Of mood which lay upon his countenance,

' Then would you say the maiden found therein
Help to reach higher than herself when bowed
She pours before that face her heart in prayer?'

'I think she would,' she said, 'and wherefore not?
Is every longing for a nobler will
Or purer heart or every cry for love
Sent up to heaven, to turn responseless back
When poured from hearts that know not how to pour
That prayer in fashion which is rightfullest?'

'But what in that Madonna's face affords,'
Said Flaxton, 'to her votary that return?
Is it the face alone, the shape, that speaks
In answer to the yearnings stretched thereto?
Or is it face together with the name :
And that she therefore sees therein pourtrayed
What in the mother of her Lord her church
Has taught her is that mother's grace and love?
Do face and lineament alone suggest
And wake the thrill which lifts the heart to give
Obeisance thus?'
                    The maiden then, '''Tis more,
The face has more than form, a veil of thought
And light of smile and sweetness on the lip.'

' But these,' he said, 'are form and what but form?
Expression is but form ; and thought and love

Traced on the face are phases of its form.
And form commands, I grant, the mind to kneel
In reverence of its perfectness, but fails
To woo the adoration of a love
Which mates the reverence, save it meets therein
Suggestion that is something more than form :
Hearts seek for something more, which finding there
They own the longings of desire fulfilled
By offering up the worship which is love.'

'It is the rule you give,' replied the maid,
'And as the rule I grant it truth, but rule
May hold within its field what offers not
At first itself as held within the rule ;
As rocks stand up to break the level flat
Of grassy mead, and seem not of the mead,
Yet are of that which underlies its sward.'

'I know,' said he, and with a husk which caused
The maiden's eyes to look upon his face—
And at the look the husk increased—
                                    'The rule
It was I gave, but will you let the rule
Suffice for me if it suffice to wake
Worship within that bends its knees to you?'

A moment—and the glitter of her eyes
Showed that her thought was sallying forth to meet

With lance of playful keenness such attack ;
But in the husk and in the eye which fell
Before his voice had struggled to the end,
And in the paleness spreading o'er his face,
She read the earnest meaning of his heart ;
Her heart held back the thought, and gave reply,
'Suffice for me what will suffice for you.'

Firenze, O Firenze beautiful !
A dream of wonder in a land of dreams
Of beauty.   Light was more than light that lit
The parting view of Arno's palaces,
And hue was more than hue and shape than shape
Bathed in the glorifying dream of love.

Ring out, O bells, ring out, ring out, and clear
Utter in clang that stirs the marriage morn
With winged vibrations flung from off your tongues
The strain that swings its thrilling hope afar.
Ring hope, long hope, and love as long as hope,
And life-long love.   Ring hope and life and love !

Ring out and clear—ring out, O clanging bells,
In mingling accents of melodious tongues
Swung speaking with the lingering din that clings
Within its hollow haunt of ivied tower ;
Ring life, long life, and love as long as life,
And love-long joy.   Ring life and love and joy !

XXI

'THE LIGHT AND HIM'

'COULD it be thus? And could the cause be this?'
    The Priest it was who spoke; in Flaxton's home
Talking with Flaxton's wife about the past
And their first meeting and the band of friends
The living and the lost. It was the spring,
Cold with late eastern winds, whose stinging scorn
Breathed their secureness of triumphal cold
Through all the genial ardour of the beams
Of May's unclouded sun. The past gone o'er,
Then their talk turned to Belford's noble death
And to his widow and his infant child,
And to the help the living on the dead
In her that lived as his bestowed; and love
Living beyond the limit fixed by death.
And word escaped the lips of Flaxton's wife
Of offering unaccepted, made by Wake
Unto her sister's heart, whereat the Priest
Spake to her of the love whose secret spring
In Runimont he only late had learnt

From his pale lips and lowly uttered words,
That came with ending of a lustrous smile
Which lit the face and gemmed the tear-dim eye.

But Flaxton's wife let fall upon her knee
Her busied hands and knitted web she wrought,
And turned her eyes of wonder on the Priest,
That filled a moment later with the hue
Of earnest grief, ' My sister's heart,' she said,
' Gave not to Wake because it could not give
The love it felt for Runimont alone.'

The hand of man, by pressure on a stud,
Can start the complex series diverse-tongued
And diverse-limbed and diverse in event
Of manifold machine. Is there a hand
Behind the fateful rule of things that moves
The complex inter-working of the hearts
Of men? And is there One who moves the hand
And views with smile the dire complexity
Of love and grief that comes resultant forth?

Or is the fateful rule of things the work
Of One who loves and stirs in those He loves
That which alone love's Io-torture spurs—
Torture that goads to sweetness seen afar,
But kept like mirage-stream beyond approach—

The high creations of the heart and mind.
So that in hearts enthralled by ceaseless pain,
The love that loves as other love loves not
Builds, homeless, for the thoughts of men a home ;
Sings, sad, the strains which give men's sadness cheer ;
And from the dark pours dreams that thrill with light.

'T is Love that works the fateful course of things—
Thus Faith, which comes when Reason faints, would say—
And bids the weary struggler struggle on
And bring to high effect the toil begun,
Whose lowmost stones were else the whole result—
Despair's—a crumbling base of pile mislaid.

‘ But only here and there that Io-pain,
And all the grief that wrings these human hearts,
Have power to bring their effort to effect ;
If it be Love which works behind the whole,
And scatters grief upon the souls of men,
That Love then works a wreck whose thought appals
If this alone be its resultant fruit—
One useful grief in many millioned waste.

‘ One useful grief in many millioned waste.’
Thou sayest this whose vision hath no power
To pierce beyond the outmost face and reach
The workings of Creation's inner soul !
What thing amid the whole of Nature gives

Into thine hands the secrets of its all?
Is *place* the thing it seems, and thou art sure
It hath no meaning other than that one
Thou graspest? And is *time* for thee alone,
Formed only for thy mental picturing,
And nought to any thing but only thee?
Does *light* unto the vision of thine eyes
And outer sense reveal its inner self,
So that thou seest it thus the thing it is?
And doth the *song* which through the air afar
Rolls its increasing spheres of wavy length,
Do nought but speak its music to thine ears?
Thou knowest of a mission but to thee,
Is that a warrant that it hath no more?

But what the canvas of thy mind can hold—
Thine own conception's painting—thou dost deem
Their nature and their essence and their whole!

And thou, because thou *seest* one grief alone
Give hue of sweetness in the endless throng
Of griefs, wouldst class the countless throng as waste!

Be still till more is thine to know, or take
That lamp to light the dark, which unto Him
Whose fate was hardest of the race of men
Sufficed to work His daring scheme of love,
Wherewith to bring back hope and joy to man :

A faith in love when love had seemed crushed down,
A faith in power that is but endless love,
When that divine conception lay, it seemed,
A helpless wreck beneath the feet of men.
Faith lit the Heart which broke upon the Cross,
What faith sufficed for Him, suffice for thee.

Once more there came the duty-call that spake
This time with voice of omen to the Priest,
Who with foreboding heart felt his thoughts driven
From the clear sunshine of their peace to dark,
And grief wailed on monotonous through the dark.

Wake's was the hand that penned the message 'Come,'
And Wake was where the message winged for flight
Set forth—the room wherein the gasping form
So dear to him and to the Priest was laid,
So near to utterance of the words which *are*,
But do not say ' farewell.'
　　　　　　　　　Two days agone,
To suffering woman helpless, help bestowed,
And long necessity of patient stand
While the wind shivered through his weakly frame
Brought fierce assault upon the hold of breath,
And fevered fury carried all with rush.

And night, in hours of chattering dream, revealed

The secrets of the silence and the past :
A name in piteous accents or in tone
Of cooing love repeated o'er and o'er—
A name that made the face of Wake, who watched,
Turn pale—but paler when the Priest told all.

And well it was to tell. The grief that rose
From great to greatness of a hundredfold,
But had thereby the chance to speak its thanks,
And sate by words from living lips to ears
Which heard, its longing thanks : that grief were else
The life-enduring cry of vain regret,
Uttering from bitter morn to bitter night
Unchanged its useless echo, answered not
But by itself. 'Would I had had the chance
To tell him of my grief, my love, my thanks,
And feel he knew them ; it were anodyne
To quell the passion of this moveless pain !'

The morn came slowly creeping on the dark
As if continuing the night and dream ;
A day that not in clouded sky nor sun,
But in the hearts and thoughts, seemed lengthening out
The night, and paling with the weltering cloud
Of grief the thoughts of those who watched the sick.

Short snatches came of sleep, and then he woke

Delirium-free.

       'O Runimont, O friend,
Dear always—dearer now I know the grief
That bound your heart in love the more to me.
How willing would I change my lot for yours
If, dying, I to you the years could give,
You have foregone for happy love and me,
If, dying, I could give the hope of life
And years of love to compensate the past.'

    But Runimont, with feeble hand outstretched
And laid in Wake's, and look of pain replied,
'Nay, have my lips revealed with traitorous words
The secret that I thought I kept barred in
From stealing forth to you?'

                 'Delirious words,'
The Priest replied, 'made needful all the tale,
Nor let your heart be grieved that it is told,
Nor let it take amiss the news I bring—
News that but yesterday 't was mine to know
She whom you love denied her heart to Wake
Because her heart, you knowing not, was yours.'

    Awhile his eyes grew wide with open stare,
Then trembled on his lips some soundless word,
And then his eyes half closed and open lip
Kept silence. Then his brain had passed the swoon

Of pain. He looked to Wake. Appeal and love
Were in the look.
    'Oh, Wake . . . if she were here. . . .
Wake, is it what I have no right to wish?'

Wake's eyes were dim and throat too full for voice,
But to the Priest with look that was request
Turning, he had no need for word to speak.

And going forth, the Priest to Flaxton's wife
Revealed the wish and the event that brought
The wish.
   And then one night, a night that buoyed
The sinking life of Runimont with hope,
Which else that night had sunk in deep of death;
And with the morn she came so long adored,
So loved. The worship of his dying eyes
Turned to her face, and o'er his features spread
A hallowed light of reverent joy. As one
Who sees the hope that years of toil had reached,
But sudden reached, when never sign had told
The nearness of the joy expectancy
With cold procrastination had denied,
And kept denial o'er and o'er in front—
So rapt in sudden bliss he took her hand
That trembled in the trembling wherewith death
Shook his, and placed it to his lips, then spake
With feeble sound that had but scanty strength

To reach the ears of him whose ears it claimed,
And, taking by the hand his friend and her,
Between his hands placed theirs, and looking love
He murmured in low accents what was prayer
That ceased in weakness. Then his hand, that fell
In act of reaching, to the Priest he stretched,
Who took the hand which made its new attempt
To reach its aim ; and felt its trembling guide,
Until upon the hands of Wake and her
It lay. Attempted movement of his lips
Ceased in the sequent weakness, and awhile,
His eyes half closed, he lay and did not move.

But in a little time his eyes stood wide
With glow as of serene surprise that broke
Into a triumph-smile of joyous love.
'The light—and Him,' he said, and then the fire
Left the pale eyes, and on the sunken face
Came the cold silence of eternal peace.

Hand-written, and the last that on the leaves,
Corrected by the careful hand that wrote,
Stood shaped to last expression this, the Priest
Found in the book by Runimont bequeathed,
As token to him of his love in death.

' Beneath the sunset's crimson stain the wind

With moan of longing, moan of long regret
Utters the wail which shakes the shuddering pines;
And on the streaming air torn clouds their forms
Diffuse and helpless pour and cross the glow
And kindle into rapture, and awhile
Thrill with the light which will be theirs no more.
And eastward gloom in shapeless shroud enrobes
The might of mountains, and the rising night
Lays inky shadow on the gloom. Thereto
My upward way with stern persistence turns;
The unknown path unto the home unknown.

'And darker grows despairing eve that now
Hath lost her splendour of triumphant fire,
Too soon. The glimmering fragments of the heaven
Are blotted out by dark of storm that blacks
The dark of night. And now the wailing wind
Turns wail to hissing, and the dark is filled
With swirling sleet that stings with bitter stroke,
And stuns the torrent's roar beside the path.

'And now again the stream outroars the storm
And dim white quiverings, eddies of its foam,
Seen through the dark as dimmest haze rush by,
And ceaseless beats the torment of the rain
Which swells its flow. How far away is light?
And rest and shelter? Upward still and up
I push my ever-slowing way. For me

Night will not end in lucent joy of morn,
But in a dreamless dark, whereunto dream—
The feeble shadow of what once was thought—
Will guide and hold its torchlight dying low.
But may that dream reveal His form whose voice
Commanded all the unknown path, and led—
Himself unseen—the way through all before.'